ROYAL LINES

Boston Rebels, book 4

RJ SCOTT

V.L. LOCEY

Love Lane Books

Copyright

Royal Lines (Boston Rebels #4)

Copyright © 2022 RJ Scott, Copyright © 2022 V.L. Locey

Cover design by Meredith Russell, Edited by Kathy Krick

Published by Love Lane Books Limited

ISBN - 9781785645891

All Rights Reserved

Royal Lines (Boston Rebels, 4)

They're setting fire to the sheets, but a romance between an out and proud hockey star and a reformed playboy prince could end up burning them both.

Marquis Miller might be one of the NHL's best players, single, wealthy, and open about his sexuality, but he knows his future lies in taking over the reins of the family's multimillion-dollar company after retirement. Jumping on the family jet, he heads to Europe, tasked with schmoozing a prince into accepting his company's bid on a significant castle renovation. Assuming he'd encounter a dusty old monarch well into his dotage, Marquis is stunned to find out that Kaleb is a young, sophisticated, beautiful man with an impressive work ethic, to-die-for eyes, and a certain flair that captures Marquis's attention.

Dragging the royal palace into the twenty-first century is one battle after another for the king's youngest son. Juggling renovations, his royal duties, and attempting to reverse his former playboy prince reputation is impossible when everyone keeps dumping problems in his lap. His chaotic life takes yet another turn when an American hockey player arrives at the castle to discuss a renovation project. Marquis is the antithesis of Kaleb's newly minted, responsible outlook on life, a jock, a player, willing to take chances. Although the forbidden sex is hot, Kaleb is not ready to turn on his family responsibilities for a pretty smile and a smart mouth.

For both men, family is everything and romance will always come in second until they open their hearts to love.

Dedication

To my family who accepts me and all my foibles and quirks. Even the plastic banana in my holster.
VL Locey

Always for my family.
RJ Scott

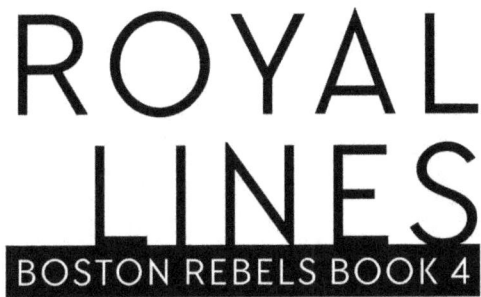

ROYAL LINES

BOSTON REBELS BOOK 4

RJ SCOTT &
V.L. LOCEY

Love Lane Books

ONE

Marquis

"SORRY, BROTHER," I HEARD TO MY LEFT AS THE BED shifted, waking me from a solid sleep.

Rubbing my eyes, I rolled to my back, the morning sun bright as it flooded my smoky gray and slate blue bedroom. You'd think I'd be more in tune with early morning wakeups, given that I had to be at the barn at the crack of dawn in season. Mornings had never been my thing. Even when I was younger, Dad had one hell of a time getting me up for school.

"S'kay," I mumbled as I sat up, the smooth sheet gliding down my chest to puddle in my lap. I truly hated mornings. Although this one wasn't too bad. Blinking into consciousness to observe Deandre Benson, wide receiver for the Detroit Mustangs, welcoming the day in his birthday suit wasn't the worst way to kick off the day. Six foot four inches and well over two hundred pounds of prime man slipping into his sexy AF yellow briefs could make a certified morning hater like me smile. We'd hooked up last night after the fundraiser for the Charles H.

Wright Museum of African American History. Being the only two Black LGBTQ athletes—that the world knew of because, trust me, there were more—that called Detroit home, we knew each other. We hooked up occasionally, nothing serious, when the opportunity struck. Like it did last night.

"Got an early morning golf game bullshit thing for ESPN." He jumped into his slacks, the tuxedo trousers gliding up thick thighs to an ass you could bounce a quarter off. The man was shredded. Not that I was a slouch mind you. I worked damn hard to keep myself in top shape. I had a reputation to uphold. Best dressed and most available gay bachelor player in the NHL three years in a row. Thank you very much. Course they could have dropped the gay part as I was pan, not gay; and why did they need to tag a label to every fucking thing a queer man did? Did the press shout "Hat Trick for Straight Hockey Player?" No, they did not. Shaking off that tiny bitch, I gave Deandre a sleepy smile. "You hockey players are lucky that no one in America cares about your game," he added.

"Suck my dick. Oh wait, you did that last night," I fired back. He snorted, tossed his dreads over his shoulder, then shrugged into his dress shirt. "I have an iron," I said then pointed to the wrinkles in his shirt.

"Nah, I'm good. Just going home to change into golf clothes. You going to be around next weekend? There's a party at Lou Kingsley's place out on Lake Sinclair. Asshole owns a massive riverfront property. Lots of cool people there."

Shit, that sounded like a blast. Lou Kingsley owned the

Detroit Yellowjackets, the MLB team that was ripping shit up in the Central Division. Lou was famed for his outrageous get-togethers.

"I'd love to." I sighed, then kicked off the covers just so Deandre could get a gander at my morning wood. His sleek eyebrow arched when he saw my erection. Yep, you're leaving this for golf, dumbass. "But I have to fly to some Swiss Miss hot cocoa country to talk pipe fittings and bidets with some old relic of a duke. Or is he a marionette?"

"That's marchioness, you fuckwit. A marionette is a puppet. Seems you'd know them royal terms as you're a marquess."

"Spelled differently. I'm like a Mercury Grand Marquis. Flashy, sexy, and one of a kind."

"Yeah, you're flashy all right." There was no lie detected. I am damn flashy. He padded over on bare feet, and gave me a kiss on the lips. "Got to roll. Call me sometime. Last night was fun."

"Will do."

I gave him a wink and watched him as he left my bedroom, shiny black dress shoes in his hands. Yawning widely, I lifted the white silk robe from the armchair in the corner, slipped it on, and went to use the bathroom. After a quick piss and a hot shower to wash the smell of sex away, I made my way through my condo, opening the drapes as I moved from the bedroom through the living room, past my home gym, and then into the kitchen. Exposed brick warmed by the early summer sun greeted me. I sailed to the Keurig on the slate marble countertop, popped in a pod of dark roast, and went on a search for my phone. Which I eventually found back in my bedroom, lying just in front of the cherry wood wardrobe that my aunt Celeste had found for me when I moved into Jackson Locust Condominiums four years ago. Auntie C had a keen eye for antiques and interior design. The woman knew how to turn out a home. Shame she didn't know how to give birth to kids that weren't fucking wastes. Rough but true.

If my cousins weren't all fools, I'd be able to enjoy my summers off. Yeah, we should be hunkering down into the playoffs now, but an insanely good New York team knocked the Rebels out in the first round. So now I had all kinds of time to spend at home attending galas, playing on yachts with rich, horny socialites of both sexes, and traveling to warm climes to shop, party, and buy clothes. But no. Because of Huey, Louie, and Dumbass—aka Jarell, Jamie, and Jordan, my aunt and Uncle Mike's half-baked sons—I had to fly over to the Kingdom of Norstoe and supervise a castle refitting.

I'd seen pictures of the old fortress overlooking a fjord. They should push the bitch into the cold, dark Scandinavian waters ASAP, then have a shiny new tower built in its place. I mean, I appreciated history and all. I lived in a building that was built in 1910. But this place had good bones and lots of amenities, like electricity and plumbing. Did those janky ass castles even have toilets, or would they expect me to use a chamber pot while I was there?

You're the plumbing man.

No, I'm not. I'm a hockey player. Dad and Uncle Mike are the plumbers.

You're the heir apparent, Marquis, so get used to it.

You're going there to make sure the old place gets all the toilets and piping it needs once Archduke Reginald the Seventy-Fifth or whatever signs on the dotted line.

If they have goats, I am out of there.

Of course, they have goats. They're in the mountains. Like maybe the Alps, I bet. They have goats out the ass, beer steins, and ghosts.

I shuddered.

Fuck off with the ghosts.

They got ghosts for sure. Castle that old? Shit yeah, it's fucking spirit central. Best get the Ghostbusters on speed dial, M.

I hate you.

"Can we brew faster?" I asked the coffeemaker just to shut down the snide voice inside my head.

It gurgled in reply, then burped out another stream of coffee. Were the needles due for a cleaning again? I'd leave a note for Janice, my housekeeper. After the brewing was done, I carried my cup to the patio, tossing the doors wide open to breathe in the fresh scent of Detroit. Mm-hmm. Smell the racial disinvestment, dilapidated public schools, and marginalized minorities being gentrified out of their homes.

This was why Black men like me needed to not only stay and live in Detroit, but to fight for it. My dad and uncle came from nothing with just a dream and a secondhand storefront. They built that rundown plumbing store over on Amos Avenue into Miller & Miller Plumbing, an international company that raked in millions in capital per year. I'd not suffered terribly in the grip of poverty. Well, not for long anyway. By the time I was old enough to grasp what being poor, Black, male, and queer in this country meant, we were no longer poor.

We were still Black—and I was still queer—but we were moving up. Just like the Jeffersons, only with no laugh track when shit got ugly. And it did. From the first time I tried on skates, there had been racial taunts. They'd hurt. They still hurt, but as I got older, faster, and stronger, I got tougher. Now when someone threw something nasty at me, I took them down to the ice. That generally ended the hate. Not always, but generally. I'd not heard a racial or homophobic slur in quite some time. Yay for progress. Didn't mean they weren't said, mind you, only that the slugs who said them were more careful.

From my red brick building that looked out over the city, as well as the tiny little walled-in vegetable garden for the condo residents, I enjoyed the sight of my hometown.

Old Mrs. Kinley, the oil shipping magnate's mother-in-law, was out tending her newly planted tomatoes. She looked up and waved, diamonds glittering in the morning sun. I lifted my mug in greeting, my sight going back to the city of steel as I readied myself for my final meeting with my father and uncle before I flew off to Heidi Land. If anyone mentioned lederhosen, I would lose my shit, hand to God.

ARRIVING AT THE ANTIETAM OFFICE CENTER DOWNTOWN, I pulled into the executive parking area, cut the engine, and waited for the valet to come dashing out from his little cubicle.

"Morning, Mr. Miller," Juan said as he opened the door of my cherry red Bugatti Veyron for me. "Sure is a fine day today. Are you going up to see your father?"

"I am," I replied, sliding my long legs out of the ridiculously expensive sports car. "He here already?"

"Yes, sir," the gangly young Latino replied as I dropped the keys into his sweaty palm. The kid got more excited over this car than he did over any of the sexy men or women that I'd brought to the tower for parties or fundraisers. Never hurt to have something beautiful on your arm. "He was here at seven a.m., as always."

"Of course, he was. Uncle Mike here yet?" I reached back into the Bugatti for my hat. Dapper men wore hats. That was just the way of it, and I was, as the world knows, one dapper son-of-a-bitch.

"Not yet, sir. Did you want this washed today?" He wet his lips in anticipation. Taking the Bug to the carwash meant he could drive it on the road and not just to my parking spot a few hundred feet away.

"Sure. And get them to do the interior too. I'll need it back by noon so I can get to Riverdale on time for the first summer street hockey game for my team."

"I'll make sure they have her smelling sweet as that model you had with you last weekend for the stockholder's fete," he replied with a wink.

"Ah yeah, Lynette. She did smell like heaven." I tossed him a randy wink, then walked to the elevator. The sounds of downtown Detroit were barely heard so far underground. With my gray Fedora set on a jaunty angle, I swept into the elevator and tapped the button for the fortieth floor. While riding up, I checked social media, took a selfie of my fine self, and posted it to IG.

#feelinggood #lookinggood #blackandqueer #detroitproud

I'd no sooner seen the first hundred little hearts appear when we were at floor number forty. Stepping out of the elevator, I looked around the massive welcoming center for Miller & Miller Plumbing. We occupied the entire floor of the tower. Glancing to the left, you could see the Ally Detroit Center. Out the other bank of windows, more skyscrapers filled the view.

"Morning, Mr. Miller," Martina called as she rushed up to greet me with a smile and a cup of hot cocoa. My father's personal assistant was efficient as hell. Cute too. And sadly married. "Sly said you'd be showing up soon. Can I get you anything from Blue Swan?"

"No, thanks, I'm good. I have to watch my weight." I patted my flat stomach. Sweets were a weakness of mine, and the Blue Swan had the biggest cinnamon buns in the state. "How's Dad today?"

We started walking, passing office after office, several meeting rooms, and a staff lounge with a few upper management types in their Hugo Boss suits, all sipping coffee. Fifty percent or more were POC, which always made me puff up with pride. Miller & Miller didn't just talk the talk, we walked the walk.

"Shaky," Martina replied, giving me a quick peek of blue eyes through golden hair.

"Figures. I'll talk to him. Anything else I need to know before I enter the lion's den?" I asked, taking a sip of rich hot chocolate as we rounded a corner and entered the outer area of my father's office. A new receptionist sat behind the glass desk. His name was Philip. Sweet little twinky sort who had big needy green eyes, red hair, and skin like cream. He'd only been here a week or so, but the come-hither looks were unmistakable. And I was certainly interested. I did not discriminate when it came to my lovers. If I found them appealing personality-wise, as well as attractive, then I was willing to get to know them better. Gender had nothing to do with who I took to my bed. If you caught my attention, it was game on.

"He doesn't have his cane," she added as we stopped just in front of the wide wooden double doors with the large M & M logo engraved into the oaken portal.

"Of course, he doesn't," I huffed, gave her a weary look, and pushed into Sly Miller's inner sanctum. The room was impressive. Lots of dark wood, fine art on the walls, and carpet so plush you could lose your Pomeranian in it. Dad sat behind a walnut desk the size of a lunch truck. His sharp gaze came up when Martina and I entered.

He was still a striking man, even if Parkinson's was giving him a bit of a stoop. He'd always been whipcord lean, for which he liked to credit his days as a long-distance runner in high school, as well as incredibly straightforward. He said what he meant with little regard for how his direct ways impacted those around him. Since his diagnosis four years ago, and my Uncle Mike's stroke two years later, both twins were growing more and more surly with age. Which was understandable. Both were—or should be—in their primes at a mere fifty-two years old. Fate was not kind to the Miller family. Cancer took my mother when I was four and had ravaged my Aunt Celeste.

She had survived her battle with breast cancer, thank God, and now cared for her husband, my father's brother, full-time with the help of an aide. So yeah, I was on the list for about a million medical conditions that would probably have me in the ground by age fifty. Might as well live life to its fullest now was my philosophy.

"Morning, son," Dad said as he pushed himself to his feet, then wobbled a little.

"You looking to take a header through that damn wall of glass behind you or what?" I barked as Martina slipped out on silent, but fashionable, tan Louboutins that went well with her taupe summer dress. My eye for fashion never closed. "Where's your cane?"

"It's over there in the umbrella stand," he replied, then dropped down into his chair with a whoosh of air. "I don't need it when I have something to hold on to. Also, the glass is thicker than your head, so no need to worry about me crashing through it."

"Mm-hmm." I snapped the cane out of the stand and carried it over to him, hooking it over the arm of his office chair as I bent down to kiss his cheek, the familiar scent of Ralph Lauren Polo enveloping me. I was more a Versace Eros man myself. "Did you take your pills?"

"Yes, stop badgering me." He waved a trembling hand my way. "Mike isn't coming. He's having a bad day."

"Okay, that's fine." I sat on the edge of my father's desk, my sight on his shaking hands. He caught me looking, then frowned. I quickly glanced out at Detroit hustling and bustling outside. "Why am I here this morning then?"

"I'm not sure you call this morning, Marquis. It's nearly noon."

I peeled off the light jacket I'd worn over a casual shirt and slacks. Dad always had his office thermostat set on inferno.

"It's not even eleven, so it's still morning. What am I doing here?" I repeated as I glanced down at him. He gave me that paternal look that told me I was walking a fine line. I knew that look well.

"I wanted to go over your notes for the Norstoe trip." He slid his reading glasses onto his wide nose, daring me to offer to help with a glower.

"Notes?"

His lips flattened. Well shit, now I'd done it. "Marquis, you can't go into something this big without doing your research on the job, the country, and the monarchy that you'll be dealing with."

"I do better when I have to think on my feet. That's why I had the second most power play goals in the league this year." I gave him my patented charming as hell smile. It had no effect.

"This isn't hockey, Marquis, this is a multi-million-dollar contract that will propel Miller & Miller into one of the leading plumbing outlets in Europe. But only if things go well. You can't go skating into Norstoe with your fancy clothes and bullshit grin like you do everything else."

I rolled my eyes. That comment stung. It always did. "What's there to know? I wine and dine this old duke or whatever until he signs on the dotted line. Then, I supervise the ordering of the plumbing fixtures, the delivery dates, and anything else we can help with. It's not that hard. I'll do my job."

"We have to take this seriously. I am not willing to let our reputation be shit like our closest competitors are. We won't use substandard equipment like Parson Wells, for example. We won't cut corners like them, so don't sell our quality based on bullshit promises."

As if *I'd* resort to shady practices. I'm Mr. Honesty. Again, I resented the implication.

"Have you even looked up the royal family of Norstoe on your fancy iPhone?" He was an Android man. We tended to be at odds about a lot of things, not the least of which was our cell phone preferences.

"Not really." I folded my arms over my chest and crossed my ankles. Dad's jaw tightened. Getting upset wasn't good for him I was sure. "Fine, I'll look up the king and queen of Norstoe. On my iPhone."

He grumbled under his breath. I chuckled then did a search online that netted me a boring page about lineage and what-nots before taking me to images of the—wow. Who the hell was the sexy bastard with the twinkle in his eye?

"That's Prince Kaleb," Dad interjected into my drool fest.

"This is Prince Kaleb?" I asked in shock as I drank in his features. Nordic for sure, with his buttermilk complexion, blond hair, and startlingly blue eyes. Damn. The man was sexy as fuck and really filled out a suit. "No shit. Well, this trip suddenly took a turn into lots more pleasurable."

"Do not flirt with the prince." I dragged my gaze from

his royal hotness. Dad was glaring up at me. "I mean it, Marquis. Do not trifle with that man. He might be the youngest son, but he's the one who makes the decisions, and he's too important to lure into bed then toss aside as you do every other person you meet."

"I don't toss everyone aside. I just haven't met anyone who made me want to keep them around for longer than a night. That's not on me. That's on them. Besides, this headline from a few years ago says he's a typical playboy prince. Oh, and he's gay."

"Marquis, if you romance that man, then break his heart, I will disown you. After I kick your ass. My hands might shake, but do not think that I can't tan your backside if I need to."

That made me snigger. Then I looked from the old article about Kaleb to my father. Yikes. Yeah, okay, he was not kidding around.

"Fine, I promise I will not romance the prince and break his heart," I vowed and crossed my heart as any good ex-scout would. Dad seemed placated for the most part. And I honestly made a promise. I'd make sure to let the hot as hell prince know it was just a summer fling. No strings and emotional attachments. Once the job was done, I was gone and back to the States. Nothing would come of it other than some intense orgasms along the Rhine. Did the Rhine run through Norstoe? Shit. I really needed to do a bit of reading.

And maybe find a map of Europe.

TWO

Kaleb

Up until two years ago, I didn't have a care in the world. Of course I have all the restrictions of being a prince including a permanent security guard, Chloe, who followed me everywhere. She was cool, we were friends, and she turned a blind eye to most of what I did as long as I stayed safe. Back then, I had to deal with world's worst paparazzi trailing me, and had kiss-and-tell stories coming out of the woodwork; plus, not one or two, but *three* paternity claims. Still, even with all of that, I never really worried about any of it. I actually played with the paps, concocting exciting escapes from wherever I was holed up, just to avoid them. One of the plus points was constant access to sex, and I never cared if any man wanted to spill the beans about whether I was good in bed.

In fact, I had everything that a rich young privileged man could wish for. The youngest of four children of an ageless queen who'd inherited the throne from her father, with money to do whatever I wanted, and a lifestyle that many would envy. I wasn't anywhere near inheriting the throne. Hell, I had my brothers Eirik and Rune, and my, older by a few minutes, twin Elsa—my parents' only daughter—all in the line ahead of me. And best of all, with this freedom to do whatever I wanted, I could have any man I desired—and believe me, I desired a *lot* of different men. In hindsight, Chloe had to see an awful lot of me sexing it up. No wonder she retired early to Aruba.

But on a single blue-sky morning twenty-three months ago, when security knocked at my hotel suite in Milan, everything changed.

My father was dead in a car accident along with his girlfriend-of-the-week. Losing Father didn't impact the throne in any constitutional way—after all, Mother was the queen, and my father, Prince Morten, had been her regent, the result of an advantageous marriage that had never really known love. Still, losing her husband had people looking at my mother, who strong as she was, suddenly appeared vulnerable to time. Not only that, but she had to publicly mourn a man she'd grown to hate. The fragility of life hit my entire family. Honestly, it hit the entire country of Norstoe.

I'd come home immediately, not to honor my father, whom I didn't give a shit about, but to be there for my mother and siblings. After having ten years of freedom, I grew up overnight and assumed my royal responsibilities. Was *that* why Chloe left or was it because I'd just become boring, and she missed the halcyon days of running from anyone who wanted a piece of Prince Kaleb of Norstoe. I was the confidant of every person in this family who felt as if I had experienced enough of the world to actually help them. I had no clue what to say to Eirik about being king because I wasn't the heir apparent, and I didn't have the pressure to find a partner, get married, and pop out a couple of kids to carry on the royal line. Mother *had* implied it might be time for me to settle down, and she'd even picked out another prince, Antoni, from a bordering country who was bi, out, and cute, but so not for me. We'd kissed once, Antoni and I, and it had been like kissing my brother. We'd agreed it was a no, but then, gay princes were few and far between, and perhaps we shouldn't be so picky.

With a degree in history, the queen—Mother—figured fixing the broken bones of our home was the role I should take on. I didn't get drunk again, stopped all the one-night stands, and overnight, I became sensible as fuck. I had to because no one else was doing it.

Eirik, the eldest of the four of us, sunk into an existential crisis over being the king in waiting when it hit him how short life could be. Not only that, but a week before the accident, he'd split up with his girlfriend Olivia over some leaked unfortunate photos of his naked ass with a woman who wasn't his girlfriend, and the media had loved that. No one liked gossip more than when it involved a prince in the headline.

Rune, the next in line, had his head in the clouds and spent more time in his art studio than he did around his family. Then there was my twin Elsa who'd reacted to Father's death by going off the rails in the worst way after having been the sensible one for her entire life.

Take now, for instance. It was only nine a.m. and my world had shifted because Elsa was standing in front of me, telling me that somehow she'd messed up.

"You married your bodyguard," I repeated dully, and my sister nodded and gripped my arm.

"You need to help me fix it." Her blue eyes were wide with shock.

"Did he force this on you?"

She blinked at me. "No. Jeez, this is Vincent we're talking about. I love him."

I'm floored that this is the first I'd heard about her even being attracted to Vincent let alone in love. What happened in Vegas certainly hadn't stayed there and it's at times like this that I'm over being the newly minted sensible one.

"Why did you get married?" I asked again.

"I didn't mean for it to happen this way," she repeated, and I watched in shock as tears rolled down her face. Since Elsa was our only sister, there's a strong possibility Eirik, Rune, and I had attempted to protect her from everything a little too much, but this latest escapade might be out of my reach to fix. From the moment the first person was ever mean to her as a toddler right up to Ricardo-the-ass who proposed last Christmas, my brothers and I have been a brick wall protecting our innocent, sweet sister, even when she wasn't being sweet or innocent at all. Hell, we all went too far when it came to looking after Elsa. Take for example, when she told us about the Ricardo proposal, it fell on me to talk Eirik out of hiring an assassin to take the man out for even daring to look at Elsa, let alone wanting to marry her.

I'd had to push my idiot brother up against a wall and tell Eirik in no uncertain terms that he was the *goddamn* heir to the *goddamn* throne of the Kingdom of *goddamn*

Norstoe and he needed not to say that *goddamn* shit. Then, I reminded him I was done with his crap, and that future kings couldn't skinny dip in the local hot springs, nor get the permanent undersecretary to the secretary to join him, buck naked with her perky breasts front and center of the photo. He'd backed off of the assassination idea quite quickly, but I think the random exposing of his skinny ass was part of a bigger plan to prove to the world he wasn't just a future king, even if it cost him his girlfriend Olivia. I think he wanted the freedom I'd enjoyed, and I understood that—I did—but I also wished he'd enjoy that freedom quietly where he didn't jeopardize his role in the family firm quite so much.

I know I'm a selfish bastard—he was just as entitled as me to let his royal hair down—but I wasn't sure my mom's heart could survive more scandal after the way Father's indiscretions had been exposed to the world.

My father's death appeared to be the catalyst for the remainder of my family to realize life was too short. Because every single one of my siblings was making me want to lock them in their rooms until they were over their shit.

Why was I the only one of my siblings who accepted that we were living in the twenty-first century and gossip was shit, and it stuck to any blanket, even if it was threaded with gold?

Rune might be less of a danger to the monarchy than Eirik, but you'd better believe I pushed Rune against the same wall and made both him and Eirik stand there as I lectured them about what they could and couldn't freaking say right now. I reminded them that even the closest of my friends had sold me out to the press; did they want the media to create monsters of them just to sell hits and papers? Prompting my siblings to recall this wasn't the seventeenth century, and we didn't kill anyone or throw them out of the country, seemed to be my go-to in recent conversations. Eirik was choking with the responsibility of his future, Rune was secretive and arty, and now Elsa was...

I can't even.

It wasn't like Eirik skinny dipping in the hot springs or racing fast cars on the roads around Treschow Fjord, or Rune getting drunk and going to a party dressed as Tarzan with a loincloth that kept falling off. No, what Elsa had done *was* a freaking constitutional crisis, and it was much worse.

"I love him," she said, for what must be the tenth time since she came into my office.

"But it wasn't so long ago when you said you loved Ricardo-the-ass." She'd seemed so genuine, but I'd balked immediately when she'd told me. I'd wanted to be happy for her, but I knew her too well, and anyone with half a brain could see Ricardo-the-ass, former racing driver and rumored gambling addict, wasn't the right man for her. She'd told him no, after the three of us had explained what an ass he was, and I lived with regret over what we did because there's a chance she had loved him, and weren't we all entitled to love whomever we love?

There again, maybe we'd been right if she'd done this.

She wiped away her genuine tears. "You said I couldn't have Ricardo."

"So, you went and married someone else? In Vegas!

Why? To spite your family because we did not like Ricardo for you?"

"No."

"Then why? You… you…" I ran out of words and slumped to the nearest seat, pulling myself together before I said something I regretted. Elsa had this way of getting under my skin, of pushing the boundaries, of making me part of her schemes just by virtue of the fact she was my twin.

She sat next to me and leaned against my arm, and I automatically pulled her to me.

"Because you were right about Ricardo. I never loved him because I've loved Vincent since the first day I saw him, but I didn't think it through," she whispered. "What have I done?"

"You went with your bodyguard and got married in a Vegas chapel, that's what you've done, Elsa! How in God's name did the rest of your security team leave you alone long enough? What were you thinking, and how will this even look?"

She stiffened at the last part. I know she hated being held accountable to anyone, let alone me. "I love him as much as he loves me. He's been my bodyguard for a year now, and we've been… you know… for a while now."

I closed my eyes, imagining how this was going to go down with the family, with the media, and with the country when it went public that Elsa had eloped with her bodyguard, who it seems, she'd been sleeping with. Or not sleeping, as the case may be.

"But where is he now? I don't see him standing by your side and facing this with you."

She let out the longest sigh and then poked me in the chest. "I didn't want you to kill him."

"He's former special forces," I countered. "He'd probably end up killing me!"

"I just needed to see you first so you could help me smooth things out with Mother." Her voice was so quiet I had to strain to hear her, but the words hit me hard. I was getting a reputation in this castle for figuring out everyone else's shit, and I was kind of done with it right now; fix this drama, fix the castle, fix my brothers with their issues, fix a wedding in goddamn Vegas.

"It's not just Mother we need to think about. Jesus, what about the country, what about the world?" Okay, I was losing my shit now. "How do you want me to... how do I even..."

The door opened, and the man himself—Vincent—stepped in, imposing, muscles on muscles, and pale as death. He shut the door behind him and gave a slight bow before moving to stand next to Elsa. He didn't immediately take her hand or try to show that he was madly in love with my sister, instead he was stiff and straight and stared right at me.

"Your Highness," he acknowledged, and I stood up to meet him eye to eye, or rather eye to chin, as I'd topped out at five ten, and he was easily six and a half feet tall and broad enough to bench press a car. He was eye candy to the extreme, and it seemed as if my sister and I shared a love for confidence and strength, so I couldn't fault her choice in a physical sense.

I do not think my sister's new husband is sexy. Shit, yes, I was thinking that. I seriously needed to get out and get myself laid. All this working hard on my image that I was not a playboy who warmed a different bed each night was going to go to hell because all it would take is one fine man to walk in here—a single man of course—and I'd spontaneously combust.

"Vincent."

We had a silent conversation in which I mentally berated him for being an idiot, shouted at him in my head for messing with Elsa, or falling into Elsa's plan, and then demanded to know what he was going to do next. In turn, he apologized with sad eyes, but he didn't back down.

"What do you want to happen next?" I asked Elsa, and she glanced at Vincent. He broke his stare at me to look down at her. She seemed so tiny next to him, and I just wanted to scoop her up and protect her from everything.

"I know it was impetuous," she finally said.

"You don't say," I snarked, which wasn't very princely at all and I instantly regretted losing my cool. "Sorry, I'm just…" *overwhelmed.* "Vincent, you're an honorable man, but you were working for us in a position of privilege. I hate that you know what it's like for Elsa and that she knew what she should have done, but you both thought it was okay to get married in some shitty place where people could take footage of you. We're held to a higher standard than others. There are payoffs and disadvantages to that. Yeah, sometimes I feel sorry for myself, and I know Elsa does too, but she and I, and Eirik and Rune, well, we're not *normal.* Our country expects us to act a certain way, and the world wants to buy into the fairy tale. You two single-handedly tarnished part of that fairy tale, and now we're heading into a media nightmare. You understand that, right?'"

Vincent nodded miserably, then with his shoulders back, he steadied his breathing.

"Permission to speak frankly, Your Highness," Vincent said, and I nodded because someone had to say something constructive here. "I love your sister. I'm aware I wouldn't be the first choice for her, but I do love her with all my heart." He was so intense, his eyes bright with emotion. "However, given the position I have put Elsa in…" He flushed red and stared down at the floor, and I felt about as comfortable as I would be if I were naked in a pile of pinecones. Lifting his chin, he was just as stubborn as Elsa. "If it's what needs to be done, I suggest we end the marriage, imply it was entirely on me should the news leak, and I handle the fallout for what happened. I can be out of the castle in ten, have a press release, and/or serve time in prison for taking advantage of Elsa, so it doesn't become an issue for the country that I love. However, should the queen consider our marriage valid, I will happily sign a retroactive prenup. I don't want anything from Elsa other than her love, if at all possible." He stiffened. "You have my sincere apologies, Your Highness, for following my heart, rather than my orders."

Oh. I hadn't been expecting that.

"Jeez, we're not putting you in jail." What was it with people thinking we did that!

"You'd do that for me?" Elsa interjected, and I realized she was talking to Vincent. He nodded all stoic and handsome. I could see Elsa's tears and the very moment she kind of melted into a puddle on the rug.

"I would do anything for you," he said, and she took his hand and held it tight.

She pressed a hand to her heart. "I love you…"

"I want you. All of you. I want to love you forever."

They held hands and made to leave the room. "Hang on, what about me here? What do I tell everyone? Who knows? Is this photo public?" I glanced at the image of my sister being carried from a plastic flower strewn altar by big strong Vincent, who was staring down at her, and my heart skipped. What must it be like to have someone look at another person with such devotion?

"Mother will surely already know." Thankfully, she was out of the country overnight, and at least that gave me some time.

"I called her and told her," Elsa admitted, then tilted her chin. "She says she'll talk to me when she gets here, but, Kaleb, I love you. Please help me fix this mess."

My heart melted at her plea, and I tugged her into a hug.

"Of course, I'll try to…"

To do what, I don't know, but I knew Mother was coming back this morning, though she might already be here. As my thoughts spun with all these conflicting issues, the door shut and I realized Vincent and Elsa had left, leaving me there, all alone.

Great, now I was in limbo with an elopement mess. I might be good at keeping my sister's secrets, but my brothers would see right through me, not to mention Mother who could read all the way to my soul. I stared out my office window, which was right on the corner where the west wall met the orangery. The view I had of the mountains above and the fjord below normally settled me. Today, it didn't because even though I live in a country that had every kind of beauty, all I felt was anxiety gripping my chest.

The monarchy could survive Elsa's elopement—we've dealt with worse—but the media would have a field day. Elsa would be front page news for weeks, with her relationship dissected for everyone to salivate over and more *Frozen* puns than they could throw a stick at. Not only that, but they'd re-run all the stories of the times I broke protocol. Add in Eirik's and Rune's recent indiscretions, and the four of us would be front and center and on repeat once again.

A knock startled me, and I hoped it was Elsa explaining that everything had been a big joke. Instead, it was Harald, my long-suffering building manager, PA— everything really—who stepped inside after my instant "come in." When I saw the clipboard in his hand, I knew I was in for yet another shitty five minutes because it seems that recently there was nothing but bad news.

"Morning, Harald." I tried to sound happy in case that would make things easier, but he launched into the list immediately.

"Your Highness, I'm sorry to report, but the ceiling in the annex has another crack and the stairwell leading to the king's study has subsided two more millimeters."

"You measured?" I had images of fussy, prickly Harald on his hands and knees with the tiniest of rulers, and it made me laugh. Internally, of course. One never laughs at another person in their face.

"Maintenance did that, sir," he said with a snooty tone

that spoke volumes of what he thought of the maintenance team. The team did a fantastic job of keeping this crumbling building secure, dealing with one thing after another, so I ignored his sniffy self. The weight of responsibility sat on my shoulders because it didn't matter that we had the funds, the extensive shifting of the castle was going to be the death of me. I thought he was done, but he wasn't.

"In addition, the drainage pipe from the kitchen has failed, allegedly due to root ingress, and despite assuring me that the upcoming birthday celebrations for Prince Eirik will not be affected, I feel as if this is a priority."

"Sure."

He checked his list. "We've shut the east wing rooms where the glazing in both the gold and green rooms has cracked with the movement in the aforementioned king's study, and we'll need a specialist to deal with that. I've taken the liberty of asking local businesses for quotes."

"Good."

"An update on the charity event, sir."

That has to be good news. Nothing can go wrong with that. Right? I'd pulled together a mini tournament that covered tennis, badminton, archery, hockey, and every other sport our country was well known for. We might be small, but the event, which was due to start in ten days, was surely beyond mess ups now.

"Hit me." I deflated when Harald's tight expression didn't relax.

"Two of the tennis stars have pulled out due to injury."

"Who?"

He glanced at his list as if he hadn't already memorized it. "Ernest Larsen and Gino Dahl."

"They're our headliners!" They were the only two professional tennis players that had made it anywhere near grand slam finals and had legitimate family connections to Norstoe. They were our shining golden ticket sellers, our chance to grab a slice of tourism revenue, and the reason many people would be attending.

"Okay, well, it's too late now to fix that." I decided on the spot because what the hell could I do about it now?

Harald cleared his throat and abruptly I knew this was going to get worse.

"Morten Jensen, badminton—"

"I know who he is."

"Well, he's not anyone too important, but..." Harald consulted his notes as if he hadn't already memorized everything and then inhaled dramatically, "due to commitments, he's decided to pull out and sends his regrets."

"Everyone is important," I reminded Harald, who raised an eyebrow in silent disagreement. I wanted to say it again, but he was right. The big stars were the tennis players, the ones who could pull in the visiting crowds, who would in turn fill the Norstoe Children's Charity with a new kind of income. I was a patron—it was up to me to make this work.

"I'll find someone else."

"Lastly, that American is here." He sniffed at that as well, with his nose very definitely pointing upward in a snobby assessment of whoever the man was.

He made a show of reading the name from the list, but

again, what Harald didn't know about the castle wasn't worth knowing, including all tradesmen and any other visitors to my office. Then it hit me that he was probably already aware of Elsa and Vincent and the great Vegas elopement.

Fuck, can my day get any worse?

"A Mr. Miller from Detroit, representing Miller & Miller," he said with added disdain. He didn't have a high opinion of Americans or the English or the French or anyone that wasn't born and raised in Norstoe. "I took the liberty of seating him in the orangery." I wish I didn't have to deal with the quotes and schmoozing from out of the country representatives when I'd rather the work was completed by a local, but no one that could handle the amount of work that needed to be done had come forward. We'd managed to gather together stonemasons, restorers, all the really skilled artisans, but the castle internals, the practical plumbing issues, were a headache I didn't need.

What I needed was to head over the border to my favorite club for some anonymous breath stealing sex, where all I had to worry about was getting myself off with another person as opposed to my right hand.

"Sir?"

"Sorry, yes, I'll head down." I rolled my neck, trying to release the stress there, and headed for the door, but Harald blocked my way. "Is there a problem, Harald?"

His expression gave nothing away. Instead, he stared right at me, much as Vincent had done. "It has come to my attention that Princess Elsa and her…"

"I know." Meeting his gaze steadily, I attempted to

exude confidence that I had the matter in hand. "I'm relying on your discretion at this time."

He waited a bit and then nodded. "Of course, Your Highness." He moved aside, but I ushered him out first, then locked the door behind us. Yeah, the trusting no one thing runs deep. I'd read up on Miller & Miller. I had learned twins built the company from nothing, which I'd found intriguing, given I was a twin myself. Now they were an established business with a worldwide reach and a reputation for excellence. They had to be, otherwise they wouldn't have even made it to the shortlist, which was currently down to them and one other. The remit was a complete castle refit, hundreds of thousands of euros needed to be spent. They informed us they had trusted contractors that could undertake other building works. I pulled out my phone and thumbed through the Android apps until I found search and then looked for the articles I'd clipped.

Two older guys, about my father's age, although they seemed older than him in the standard website photos. Sylvester, or Sly for short, and Michael. I had financial reports, an understanding of the enormity of what needed to be done, and most of all, I had the personal responsibility of ensuring the Castle of Light, its locally known name, made it another nine hundred years. One more pressure to handle, but I had to be up for the job, and I needed to push aside my concerns about the charity event until I had some space to do so.

I jumped the last five steps into the hallway, finally getting the chance to raise a smile as I managed a superhero landing, something my brothers and I had practiced hundreds of times after watching *Iron Man*. At least I could still do that. Brushing myself down, I then pocketed my cell and headed down the corridor to what we euphemistically called the orangery. It was actually an enormous glass ceilinged room that was previously used as a ballroom and was, now, home to plants that bathed in the bright sunlight flooding the area. After taking a short time to settle my thoughts, I pushed into the room and headed straight for where I knew Mr. Miller would be sitting, no doubt with coffee and cake. However, he was nowhere to be seen, and I stopped dead by the table, glancing around to see if I'd missed him in the tamed jungle of plants and fruit trees.

Then, I spotted him by the window, staring down at the same view I had from my office. Over the castle walls and to the mountains. From where I was standing, I could see he had an ass that I should not be checking out and legs that went on for miles.

"Hello," I announced my arrival, and he spun to face me. My mouth dropped open. Six feet, plus a few inches, of beautiful man with eyes so dark they were nearly black and close-cropped hair, he wore a perfectly fitted Armani suit and a patterned waistcoat in a mix of plum and gold, and was holding a fashionable hat in his hand. He smiled. The smile grabbed at my libido and didn't let go as I took my fill of the slim, but muscled, god with thighs I could bite into and lips begging to be kissed.

He bowed and extended a hand. "Marquis Miller," he introduced himself, and I took his hand and shook it firmly. He didn't let go. I didn't let go. There was something there. A flicker of appreciation in his expression, the tip of his tongue wetting his lower lip, his eyes widening, and I didn't have to wonder about his appreciation or his inclination.

If he could read my mind, he'd know that he ticked every single one of my boxes, and the image of him lying naked, with all that beautiful dark skin on cool silk sheets, sprawled and waiting for me, had all the blood in my body rushing south, and I was getting hard. The fuck?

"Prince…" I stopped. "I'm Prince Kaleb. Call me Kaleb."

Finally, he released my hand. I swear if he offered to fuck me, I'd be dropping my pants and leaning over the nearest surface.

"I'm here from Miller & Miller."

"Uh-huh." Words failed me, and an answering frown creased between his eyes.

"You were expecting me, I believe. Regarding your castle works?"

It wasn't the castle I was worried about right now. It was the fact I was getting an inappropriate hard-on at my first sight of this glorious man in what was supposed to be a serious business meeting. I'd never seen such beauty up close, and suddenly, I understood how my sister could meet and fall for someone in the space of a few days. Not that my heart had anything to do with how I felt. I was tired of all the shit, the worries, the stress, and abruptly, I wanted my old university days back when I could sleep with anyone I wanted.

Because, right about now, with everything whirling in

my head, the thought of Marquis Miller in my bed and fucking me into tomorrow, well, damn the consequences. Bring it on.

THREE

Marquis
_____

DAYUM!

I'd heard that old saying about how an image didn't capture the true beauty of something. I'd always thought that meant somewhere exotic, like a snapshot of the sunrise in Honolulu or the sight of the setting sun as you jetted into Toronto or spotting a Bengal tiger slipping through the dense jungles of Bhutan.

Never once did I think that old axiom could apply to a human being. We really do learn something new every damn day. Kaleb was gorgeous. Blond hair styled in a way to look as if it wasn't styled. Rakish, some would call it. I called it freshly fucked. Bright and intelligent sky-blue eyes and a neat beard of gold. He had the body of a swimmer, or perhaps a tennis player. Did I not see a photo of him at some celebrity tennis match to raise money for a children's hospital in Monaco? Or was it here in Norstoe? Shit. I should have paid more attention to the mounds of information Dad had emailed me, instead of watching _Pam and Tommy_ on the flight over. Maybe, I'd have dreamt about the sight of his long, strong legs in white tennis shorts. I had napped a lot as the Miller & Miller jet soared across the Atlantic. Shit, but the man was pretty. Almost too pretty.

Note, I said almost. There was a hint of rugged masculinity riding shotgun with his devastating good looks. My dick was no longer bored. Hell, I was no longer bored. This trip just got a lot more interesting.

The sizzle that sparked between us during the lengthy handshake—no, that was no handshake; that was a hand seduction—was still lighting up my nervous system.

"You were expecting me, I believe. Regarding your plumbing refit," I said again.

"Oh, yes. I'm sorry. It's been a day." He shook his head briefly, and I wondered what could be bad in a prince's day. Certainly, with all this privilege, he had to have things kind of easy. He probably had an official worrier who did all the worrying for him—probably an under-worrier as well.

"I feel you there. My ass is so jet lagged I had to get your man, Harald, to help me carry my backside up into the castle along with my bags." He snorted in amusement. Good. I like a man with a sense of humor. Life was too short to spend it frowning.

"I hope Harald proved to be an adequate ass carrier?"

I chuckled. Nice. Wit as well as devastatingly good looks. Also, he smelled lush and erotic. Dark spices wafted off his skin.

"He carried my ass with aplomb. Then, he helped me through security, which damn, was some intense stuff. Then, sat me down in this orangery, but I have to confess, Your Highness, I've not seen one single orange." I waved my hand at the foliage filling the sunroom.

"Oh, are you looking for an orange? We can ring for Harald to fetch you some citrus to snack on. I'm afraid we eat rather late here so—"

"Sure, I'll take an orange. There's always the concern of scurvy setting in after an overseas crossing." I winked and got a smile brighter than the sun warming the glass-walled room.

"I do apologize for our lack of oranges. We had some nasty citrus nematodes come in on a grafting of imported Valencias from Calabria last year. The royal gardeners had to destroy the twenty or so potted trees we'd had and start all over. We should have an orange in about five years." He took out his cell phone and tapped away at it. "There. I've advised Harald that you wish to have an orange in our orange-less orangery. Would you like to have a seat or take a walk through the castle to see the work that's going to be required?"

What I really wanted was to take the prince to the nearest fluffy flat surface and let him ride my weary ass until I passed out from pure pleasure. Followed immediately by a quick cuddle and about eighteen hours of sleep.

"No, hey, I was kidding about—"

A soft rap on the glass door, and good old Harald appeared with a platter that held a quartered orange, a spoon, and a cloth napkin with a fancy looking family crest stitched onto it. I blinked at the older man in shock.

"Your orange, Mr. Miller," Harald said, then bowed

ever so slightly. The orange never moved. Okay. I am impressed.

"How the hell did you get this here so fast?" I enquired as I took the dish from the building manager.

"Gustave has suffered a small injury. Nothing serious, just a twisted ankle, and since I was in the kitchen, I offered to carry the requested fruit to our guest."

"Oh? Will Gustave be okay? Tell him not to hurry back." Kaleb said all of that while I stood there with an orange on a plate, looking like a moron. I didn't really want an orange, but since good old Harald had hustled it to me, I'd eat it.

"He should return to his duties as head butler within a fortnight. Until then, we'll have to run the household on a skeleton crew as the rebuild is going to affect much of the castle. If you'd like, Your Highness, I could give Mr. Miller a tour of the castle when his jet lag is cleared. This way he could rest from his flight, and we'd be able to round up a suitable replacement for Gustave from the staff?"

"Oh, yes, of course. I didn't think of how tired you must be, Mr. Miller. Let's sit out on the veranda while you have your orange. Then, we'll have one of the footmen escort you to your room," Kaleb said, motioning to the patio overlooking the fjord sitting just on the other side of some ornate doors.

"Yeah, sure. Thanks for this, Harald." I held up my plate of oranges and got a nod from the man I had assumed was the head butler dude. Was there a proper name for head butler dudes? Damn it. That'll teach me to spend my time watching Sebastian Stan, instead of reading up on royal protocol and regal households. Still, man, it was Sebastian Stan. I regret nothing.

I'd catch on. Like I'd told my father, I was quick on my feet. Couldn't be too hard to figure out who was the butler and who was a maid. Not that I had a lot of experience with big household staffs. Even as wealthy as my family now was, we didn't have butlers and footmen or whatever. My dad had a housecleaner and cook—Rolanda —who had been with us for years. Other than Rolanda, a trio of gardeners who mowed the grounds weekly, and a pool cleaning service, that big old house in West Bloomfield was empty. When broached to get some help from someone other than Rolanda—who was as old as, if not older than, my father—Dad would scowl and snap: "Do I look like the Queen of England? The day a born and bred Detroit boy like me needs a lord in waiting to polish my belt buckle is the day I roll my Caddy into Lake Michigan and end it all."

Ah, yeah man, Americans. You got to love us.

I glanced from the now closed door to Kaleb, and my dick twitched. He was taking a long look at my glorious self. Uh-huh. There were going to be some hot nights on the old fjord.

Do not trifle with that man. He might be the youngest son, but he's the one who makes the decisions, and he's too important to lure into bed, then toss aside like you do every other person you meet.

Well shit. My father's warning rang out inside my head. Not that I planned on trifling with Kaleb. There would be no vows of everlasting love or devotion. He was into me, I could see that, and I was deep into him—damn

I wish I was deep in him—so maybe we could just come to a mutual agreement. A few weeks of mind-blowing sex, then that was that. I went back to the States, and he continued playing prince. We were both big boys with pasts filled with liaisons, while not exactly checkered, that didn't end in something binding. How would that even work? He was in Europe, and I was in the U.S. So yeah, a hot and sweaty summer relationship, then bonjour or however they said "later" in Norstoe. Did they speak Swedish? Norwegian? Norstoenian? Fuck. I foresaw lots of reading of boring royal stuff in my immediate future. Possibly after the prince and I had a tumble in his princely bedroom… damn it, now my cock was plumping up.

"Come, let's sit and talk for a bit." Kaleb threw the doors open. A warm rush of wind blew into the elegant orangery, carrying the metallic scent of the dark, deep waters of Treschow Fjord. "I thought you might appreciate seeing the fjord a bit closer. Here's a seat."

We sat down on a cement bench about fifty feet from the water.

There was a low stone wall around several flowerbeds that were just starting to burst into color. Trees offered shade for those seeking it on warmer days. May still had a chill to it here in Norstoe. My coat was more for show than actual warmth, and I shuddered just a bit as I drank in the raw, natural beauty of this country. The majestic Scandes mountain range rose up to kiss the light blue sky in the far distance as the soft lap of the fjord on dark, smooth rock soothed my travel weary soul. "In the winter the fjord freezes solid, and we enjoy a good shinny game."

My sight flew from the napkin draping over my slacks to the man sitting beside me. "You play shinny?"

"I do, yes," he replied, then smiled impishly. I liked that flash of the devil. "Do you?"

I cast a glance his way. Evidently, he didn't know who I was, just that I was there representing Miller & Miller. Interesting. I guessed he didn't know much about the NHL, plus Miller isn't an exotic name, so I shouldn't have felt aggrieved that a prince in a foreign country didn't know who I was, right?

"I know what shinny is," I demurred.

"Well, we have a team here: The Norstoe Moose. They did quite well last year. I like to play goalie when I have a chance. Sadly, we don't get to the nearby rink often enough for me to join a team as I had when I was younger."

"There's a rink near here?"

"There is a rink near here, yes."

"You're a prince, and you play hockey?"

"I play hockey."

"No shit."

"No shit," he parroted, which made me smile before taking a bite of the orange. The juice of the sweet fruit burst over my taste buds. I moaned in pleasure as juice dribbled over my lower lip. His gaze flew from a pair of swans gliding by to my mouth. His nostrils flared. My dick pulsed. I licked the juice from my lip, my sight locked with his. Right now, a Yeti could snowboard down from the fluffy white peaks and crash into the fjord with a "Cowabunga, dudes!" and neither of us would see it. "You look tired."

"A little nap will fix me right up." I placed the plate on the cold cement bench, then gave Prince Kaleb my best "you, me, and a bed soon?" simmering look. He darted a glance back at the castle, then met my hungry gaze again.

"I can show you to your room if you'd like."

"That would be most appreciated, Your Highness."

He wet his lips, stood, and pushed at the erection in his slacks with the heel of his hand. Fuck me, the man had a rack of meat hidden in those Christian Dior pants of his.

"Please, call me Kaleb."

"And you can call me Marquis," I replied, leaving my orange forgotten on the bench as I followed Kaleb like a love-sick puppy. My body was thrumming with pent-up lust that did not abate when I followed him up a spiral staircase. His ass was delicious. And knowing—or suspecting—that I might be getting a handful of it soon sent more blood rushing to my cock. It was a miracle that I didn't pass out and tumble backward down the old stone stairs due to decreased blood flow to my brain. Kaleb was chattering away as we passed ornate oils hung on the cold gray walls, telling me who each sour faced old monarch was. A Klaus this and an Olav that. Lots of Roman numerals thrown in, as well as tidbits about the eccentricities of each ruler.

"It seems a passionate nature runs in the family as my great-grandfather not only had several mistresses, but was rumored to be quite enamored of the royal librarian. Of course, a gay romance back then had to be kept a secret. Thankfully, today two men who find themselves attracted to each other can sleep with each other without fear of beheading."

I skidded to a halt at the riser, ripping my gaze from his ass to gape at him. "They beheaded people here?"

He turned, the sun streaking in through one of the tall arrow-slit windows, making his safflower hair glow like twenty-four karat gold.

"No, just a joke."

His teasing hung between us, and I lost myself in his beautiful eyes. There was no mistaking that, if we were anywhere but in a castle, we'd be dragging each other into the nearest room with a lock on the door.

I snorted in amusement. *Funny. Real funny, Your Highness.*

"So, this room on the left is the family chapel." I peeked into the small, but tidy, room that housed a few dark wooden pews, stone walls covered with tapestries, and an ornate chandelier hanging over a pulpit covered with red velvet upon which two massive gold candelabra stood, new white candles ready for the next mass. "Down the hall is Olav the Fifth's study, the queen's library and office, and the main library where my sister spends most of her time. Well, she used to, but now she's doing other things."

There was a lot of emotion in that last sentence, and I got the feeling the sexy prince was upset about something. Anyway, it wasn't my place to comment or ask, so I focused back on the tour.

Suitably impressed and a little worried, even a half-assed plumber like me could see the signs of time on the castle. Small things to be sure, but still evident. Crack lines here and there, rooms that had been closed off with signs telling visitors not to enter, plaster that was peeling and cracking.

"Do you have tours in here?" I asked then checked out a small alcove that held the bust of a woman in a crown. The nameplate said she was Crown Princess Josephina.

"Not anymore. It's not structurally sound enough in some parts to expose the public to any potential harm." I glanced up from the bust of some old dead lady to the ceiling overhead. "It's not that bad. The castle won't come down on your head, but it's best to not have people poking about. The basement where we keep the royal sarcophagi of several of our past rulers is the most popular place on the tour, but the stonework there is—"

"Wait." My sight flew from the ceiling to my guide. "You're telling me there are dead people in the motherfucking basement?" My voice may have cracked just a bit at the end of my question. I cleared my throat and tried to look cool. Shit. Had that just slipped out? Crap. I ramped up the cool. I mean, I always looked cool, but maybe super cool. Kaleb studied me with what I could only describe as subdued amusement on his handsome face.

"Yes, the bodies are kept in the royal burial chambers as is tradition. I think there are about thirty sarcophagi down there now. All are being removed though, as the water seepage from the fjord is making storing them down there impractical until the renovations are complete."

"Cool. Cool. So uhm, just as a point of interest, where the hell are you people storing the dead folk, and are they mad?" I leaned on the wall next to the bust of Princess Jo. Total nonchalance, cool as a damn cuke.

"The workmen? No, they're not mad. They know it is part of their job to—"

"No, not the workmen. The dead people. Are the dead people mad that you're moving them from their final resting places? I've seen the movies. Dead people get pissed when you move them."

He was working to hide a smile. The cheeky bastard. "No, no, they don't mind. And if they did, they could join the other ghosts that walk the castle at night."

My eyes flared. Nowhere in the emails I'd read was there one fucking mention of ghosts. I didn't do scary shit. Nope. No way. Fuck this noise. I was going to sleep in the family chapel. It was the only safe place. Ghosts. My father was going to get a nasty text about this otherworldly bullshit. Someone touched my arm. I yelped, leaped into the air, and nearly knocked Princess Jo off her plinth. Due to my being incredibly slick and possessed of quick reflexes, I saved the bust from tumbling to the hard stone floor.

"Fuck me!" I yelped, clutching Jo to my chest as Kaleb, now smiling outright, rubbed his hand up my biceps in what was supposed to be a calming way. All that touch did was reignite the desire that the ghost news had dampened. "Oh, heck, I mean." I glanced at a servant skittering past. She curtsied to Kaleb, then gave me a long awkward glance. "Heh. Jet lag always makes me skittish. I'm like a thoroughbred stallion, you know. A little jumpy, but guaranteed to give you a hell of a ride."

There, that sounded like my usual composed self.

"I'm a rather skilled equestrian," Kaleb said, his fingers biting into my upper arm. He wet his lips. My gaze fell to his mouth to enjoy the slick pink glide of his tongue over a lower lip that needed to be bitten and tugged. "Would you like to watch me ride you sometime?" His voice was low now, thick and smoky and filled with carnal pleasures.

"Now sounds good," I replied, my cock now fully back into the whole sex with the hot prince thing. I leaned in and down, as he was a little shorter than my six foot three inches. His eyes changed from a light blue to a darker shade. My dick was incredibly happy.

"Kaleb, here you are. And this must be our guest from America?" a woman called. I jerked back as Kaleb did, Princess Jo bobbling about between us. He slapped a hand to the bust to pin it to my chest as an older woman, perhaps in her late fifties, with silver threaded short blonde hair and the same stunning features Kaleb possessed, walked up to us.

"Mother, yes, this is Marquis Miller of Miller & Miller. I was just showing him to his room," Kaleb calmly replied. "Mr. Miller, this is my mother, Queen Marianne."

"Your Highness," I coughed out, passing Princess Jo to Kaleb so I could bow to the queen. "It's a pleasure. You have a lovely castle."

She smiled softly, slid her hands around Princess Jo, and placed the bust back on its plinth.

"Thank you. Harald informs me that you're one of two contractors coming to see the work required and make final bids. I hope you enjoy your stay here. Kaleb, will you join me in my office at your convenience after seeing Mr. Miller to his room in the blue wing?"

"Of course, Mother." Kaleb looked over his mother's head to give me a quick unreadable look.

"Excellent. I'll see you at dinner, I hope, Mr. Miller. I'm looking forward to hearing about the States. It's been too long since I was there to visit." She gave me a soft inclination of her head, then padded off on tiny little blue flats that nicely matched her navy slacks and white blouse.

"It looks like the riding will have to take place later," Kaleb whispered in my ear as Princess Jo eavesdropped. "When Mother says to join her at your convenience, that means to join her within fifteen minutes and bring some baked goods."

"We don't want to make the queen mad."

"No, we do not. Let me show you to your room."

He did, then said he would see me at dinner, gave me a courtly little bow and dashed off. I'm guessing to round up some baked goods and see his mother.

Sighing, my dick now thoroughly confused, I entered my room, gaped at the magnificence of the cherrywood furnishings, bright blue tapestries on the stone walls, and the patio that awaited, just on the other side of a thin door that stood cracked open to allow the fresh air of the fjord to fill the room.

I took off my hat, loosened my tie, tossed my jacket over my bags sitting neatly on racks beside a magnificent wardrobe, and sat on the edge of a huge bed. The mattress sank a good foot as a rush of floral scent rushed up to tickle my nose. The clean linens were lovely, but they didn't hold a candle to the smell of Kaleb's aftershave. What a damn shame that moment had been lost, but there would be others. Possibly after dinner. I yawned, toed off my shoes, and fell back into the bed.

With the call of swans in the air, I fell dead asleep as soon as my head hit the downy mattress.

FOUR

Kaleb

I TOOK A DETOUR AND HEADED BACK TO THE CHAPEL, pulling the door closed behind me and then banging my head on it. "Would you like to watch me ride you sometime? What the fuck, Kaleb?" What in God's name was I thinking? Elsa was wholly inappropriately married to a man she may or may not have feelings for. Eirik was in crisis over being the heir, and Rune was never here and stayed buried in his studio with his art. Worse, the damn castle—our home—was falling around my ears.

And I imagined that, somehow, amidst all of that, I could have a random fuck with a stranger who was here on castle business for no other reason than I'd got all worked up.

Pressing the heel of my hand against my stubborn erection, I willed the thing to go away. Now was not the time to channel University Kaleb, now was the time for me to be the sensible one—the man who could fix everything for everyone else. Starting with appearing in front of my mother, the queen, and explaining why I let Elsa get married. Not that I had, but I knew she'd tell me I should have known, or at least heavily imply it. Such as how I should have known the pipe in the kitchen would crack and the cellar had subsided, and hell, a million other things that I'd taken the responsibility for.

I banged my head on my hands one last time and, then, filled my thoughts with anything that wasn't Marquis Miller… and his ass… and his hands… and the smooth way he caught that bust… and the way he talked to me as if I was a regular person… and that he might have even liked me for who I was…

Fuck my life, I was getting hard again.

When I put my focus on the sewage pipe from the kitchen, that got my dick to subside and nestle in my boxers like a sleepy hamster. Only then was I ready to see Mother. I headed down the long corridor and up a flight of stairs to the royal rooms, where both parents had studies, along with interconnected sitting rooms, formal rooms, and their vast bedroom with views out over the fjord. Shoulders back, I hesitated outside the door, giving myself a little breathing room, but as I went to knock on the door, it flew open, and my mother's secretary scurried out looking as if she wanted to be anywhere else but inside that room. This did not bode well.

I slipped inside, where Queen Marianne had her back to me, staring out at today's beautiful blue skies.

"Mother," I acknowledged and bowed quickly when she turned. I crossed over to her, and she tugged me into a hug, burying her face against my chest and sighing heavily.

"I'm sorry, Kaleb," she murmured. I wasn't expecting that at all.

"What for?" I asked, and we separated so I could take the seat on the visitor's side of the desk, but she caught my arm, and instead we went outside onto the balcony and closed ourselves off from the world.

"For this to happen when I wasn't here."

"It's nothing I couldn't handle," I lied.

Queen Marianne was a beautiful woman—regal —her blond hair in a short pixie cut, and her clothes always impeccable. The very fact the royal family existed was a big part of the reason our tourism industry was so strong, and our queen was our figurehead. Visit for the mountains and stay for the castles was on the earliest advertising campaigns I remember, and we relied on the people who visited for the fairy tale.

The crumbling fairy tale.

"Elsa explained she married her bodyguard, Vincent Haugen. Do we know anything else?"

I winced. "I haven't seen official documentation, but there are photos, and I spoke to Elsa an hour ago, and she admitted it to me as well."

Mother sighed again and took my hand. "It's you they go to now. I'm proud of you," she whispered before her expression changed to what I could only describe as wistful. "Is Elsa happy? When she told me, she was scared, and I couldn't get a real sense of how she was. I just want her to be happy. Vincent is a steady man, good at his job, but is he a *good* man?"

I would assume that Vincent had already been the subject of an in-depth background clearance given his position as Elsa's bodyguard, but add in this new twist, and I would lay money on the fact that the royal guard were digging way deeper than the security check. Married to a princess, he would now be under scrutiny going back generations because God forbid he had some ancestor who wronged people in a country we were now talking to. Everything would come out as soon as Elsa's marriage went public, which was probably closer than we could imagine.

I went for honesty. "All I know is that he clearly loves Elsa."

"And what about Elsa? Does she love him?"

I gripped her hand. "He told her he would go to prison for her, accept all the blame, and I could see the love in his eyes." I glanced up at Mother and wondered if she thought I was being fanciful. She simply nodded, and so I carried on. "She loves him just as much."

"Particularly after Ricardo-the-ass," she said, and I hid my smile at the way she spoke about him. Mother using anything like the word "ass" made all four of her children snigger.

"We probably need to implement code magenta," I suggested.

Now it was her turn to smile. Code magenta was a family thing. The four of us, plus Mother, decided we needed a name for when the shit hit the fan to the point that we knew we'd be running around like headless chickens. Code magenta was a good call.

"Will you talk to her some more?" I asked.

She closed her eyes briefly, the only outward sign that she was worried. "I want her to talk to me. I won't demand to speak to her, either as her mother or as her queen, because either way, I hope she will choose to come to me. We can talk, and then I can meet Vincent officially, rather than in a security meeting. Harald is on his way to a complete meltdown, and I don't know how long we have until someone shares the photo or the news, but it will happen, and then we will lose the chance to control the narrative."

"I'm on it." I went to rise, but she stopped me and took my hand again.

"I need to talk to *you*, Kaleb." Shit. I hated conversations with my mom that started like that. What had I done now?

"Okay."

Mom touched my arm. "Mr. Miller has a very nice smile and is a fine character to represent his company, don't you think?"

I swear there had to be a catch in the question somewhere, as if Mother had opened a hole in the floor and was waiting for me to step into it. I worried at a thread on my shirt, but kept my gaze steady.

"We haven't talked finer details as yet."

"I saw the way you looked at him, Kaleb. It's the way I looked at your dad when I first met him, as if I could eat him up right there and then. I was wrong to let my sexual needs override my common sense."

"Mooother," I whined because no kid wants to think about their mother getting it on, particularly to a man who turned out to be a philandering asshole.

"Mr. Miller is a handsome man, and I can see why you were staring at him with such awe."

"I was worried he'd drop the bust," I lied.

She huffed a soft laugh. "You're my son. Don't think I don't know you. There is something about this man that calls to you right now, and compels you to watch him and want to understand him. Please be sure of what you are doing before you add to the issues you are already dealing with. Queen Annabella and I spoke again regarding her youngest son, Antoni, and we feel that a match could be advantageous." This wasn't the first time someone has mentioned Antoni's name to me, but when I opened my mouth to remind her that this was the twenty-first century, I realized there was no point and shut it again. "While I'm aware you have worked incredibly hard to clean up your image, and I'm very proud of you, I'm thinking that if you spend time with Prince Antoni, you might find him as attractive as Mr. Miller."

I didn't find Antoni unattractive, but marrying him just to boost the family and its ties with his country was so last century, and I was squarely a new millennium kind of man. As was Antoni.

"I'll take it under advisement," I grumbled, feeling as if I was betraying myself by wanting her approval. I know every child wants to make their parents proud, but I was a strong independent person who didn't need to marry for the country. Right?

"You should talk to him at your brother's party." She patted my hand and sat back.

"I didn't see his name on the invite list." And I should know because I checked it carefully. Seemed to me Antoni was being invited to a whole heap of things just to be put in my locale.

"I invited him. After all, he should learn more about Norstoe."

"Mother—"

"I just want you to know that I see how hard you've been working, but also that I worry about you being lonely."

"I'm not. I'm busy, and I'm focusing on the castle and the charity event, not to mention Eirik's birthday event soon"

"I thought Elsa and Rune were helping with that."

"Well, Elsa got married and Rune... well Rune is Rune."

She seemed troubled, but then the conversation returned to me. "So, if you are lonely and you decide to spend time with Mr. Miller, I hope you will do so with discretion. Please be aware that the contracts we are potentially entering into with his family company must be completely aboveboard. Harald explained that Ms. Wells from the London based company, the alternative bidder, will arrive the day after tomorrow, and I don't have to tell you that both Mr. Miller and Ms. Wells are to be treated fairly for the final bids."

"Of course."

"And should you *entertain* Mr. Miller, please ensure that Prince Antoni isn't aware. We wouldn't want to scare him off."

By the time I left her study, my head was spinning, and I headed straight for the one place I knew I could think. The room at the top of the east tower. It was only accessible from my bedroom, and it held a sofa and a bookcase with a power connection from below, which meant I could charge my phone, read a book, and think about nothing. As I was the only person with a key, apart from Harald and housekeeping of course, it was my little sanctuary. I sat there for a while, curled up in the corner of the sofa, my phone in my lap, and took a moment to breathe—long enough to prioritize everything going on right now. Elsa first. The birthday party next. The broken pipes and cracks after. The charity sports event came in a close fourth. And way down the list, like way down deeper than the bowels of the castle, was my instantaneous attraction to Marquis Miller.

I'm not a teenager anymore—I can handle my hormones.

My cell vibrated, and a message from Elsa popped up. *Where are you?*

I typed that I'd meet her in my office, and I was up and out of the room as soon as I pressed send. I jogged along the wide corridors, tipping my hat to a former Prince Kaleb, whose painting made him look permanently pissed, and then slid into my office and found Elsa on her own. My heart stopped. She didn't look devastated, nor was she crying, but she had her arms wrapped around her middle, and as soon as I stepped into the room, she flew at me for a hug.

"Okay, it's okay; nothing we can't handle," I lied. After all, one constitutional crisis after another is my norm right now, and I can handle any code magenta thrown at me.

"I wrote a statement," she added and pulled away. "I'm happy, and I want this marriage to work. Am I being stupid?"

Cradling her face, I pressed a kiss to her nose. "If you feel you want to try, and you really love him, well… things could be worse."

"I challenged him in Vegas and told him if he loved me as much as he said he did…" She paused and blushed. "I wanted to grab my chance to be with someone I actually wanted to be with, rather than the person I was told I was going to be with. I thought I'd always have to marry someone like Ricardo, with the aristocratic history and money that could help our family. Do you understand, Kaleb?

More than she knew.

"I do."

Mother's words about how a match with Prince Antoni could be advantageous filled my head, and I knew exactly what Elsa meant about expectations. Sometimes, the world got in the way of the best of intentions, and a person just wanted to forget the weight of everything and live a little.

Get your head back in the present. I listened to my inner voice and focused back on my sister. Then, Elsa and I worked on the press release, keeping it to a simple love story. We added some information about Vincent, who fortunately for the optics, hailed from our very own Norstoe and was the son of a lawyer; plus, he was decorated former special forces, who'd moved into private security. He wasn't rich, and inevitably the media would suggest he was social climbing and marrying Elsa for her money, but I'd thought of a fix for that, and maybe a public retroactive prenup was a good idea. Elsa was happy. When I'd looked Vincent in the eye this morning, I saw a man truly in love, and I would move heaven and earth for my sister. I called for Harald, and as he came in, he bowed to us both. He'd always had a soft spot for Elsa. In fact, the only time he smiled was when he was talking to her. He wasn't smiling now, instead he seemed wary. I guess he was wondering how magenta our most recent fuckup was, and I decided to clear the air without ceremony.

"Princess Elsa and Vincent Haugen were married in a private ceremony two days ago. Could you arrange for Elsa to be moved to a set of apartments in the east wing with a study for Vincent? He will resign from his position on her security team and will join me in working at the castle as my respected brother-in-law. All titles will follow, and so on."

"Thank you," Elsa said.

"Very good, Your Highness," Harald spoke over her. Then he turned, and I got a glimpse of his rare smile. "Congratulations, Princess Elsa. I like that young man."

She smiled back, and it was real. "I do too. Thank you, Harald."

I passed the press release to Harald. "Could you make sure this gets to the press team for immediate release? I'll pencil in a ceremony to be held at St. Martin's Chapel in, say, two months to give ample time for the country to plan. Elsa will need a ring, possibly our grandmother's, since it was expected to go to her. Also, please arrange for a trusted media source to do an interview with the happy couple."

"Very good, Your Highness." As soon as Harald left, Elsa hugged me hard and kissed my cheek. "I love you," she whispered. "I'm going to see Mother now."

Before Elsa left, I got in one last hug, and suddenly I

was alone. I slumped into my chair and massaged my temples, trying to release the pain there, and relaxed my shoulders, which were tight with stress.

I shuffled the notes on my desk, trying to concentrate on each one. The town fireworks for Eirik's celebration were in jeopardy because of health and safety concerns. Rune's credit card statement showed he was nearing his very generous limit. The crack in the wall of the gold room made the room unsafe, and the kitchen pipe fix would run twenty thousand euros minimum. I scrubbed at my eyes, attempting to still the tension headache that had begun as soon as I woke up. I couldn't deal with any more right now, so I went for one of my castle walks—the type that took me all over the castle, checking on things, talking to people, taking photos with my phone, and fixing what I could as I went.

I just wanted something to go right for once.

FIVE

Marquis

REST DID WONDERS FOR A MAN.

It seems whatever hours of sleep I'd managed sat well on me, if I did say so myself. Checking my face in the mirror after a shave and shower, I could see the bags under my eyes were greatly reduced. My tunes were playing in the room. NBA YoungBoy was rapping about having the bag, the volume nice and high.

Digging around in my travel kit, I found some eye cream that would reduce the remaining puffiness within minutes. Sure, sometimes the guys on the Rebels gave me guff over my meticulous manscaping and attention to detail, but a little extra work paid off in big dividends. I'd put my tally of dates and lovers up against any of theirs. ZZ Top was right when they sang about girls being gaga over a sharp-dressed man. It wasn't just the ladies either. Other men liked to see me looking my best when we were out.

Pulling on some slim cut black slacks that rode above the ankle, I added a short-sleeved fuchsia shirt and matching socks with a pair of brown Chelsea boots. Atop my head was a pink fedora with a matching ribbon and gold pin with a BLM black fist pin. I took one final spin in front of the full-length mirror in my room, deemed myself hot as shit, and gathered my wallet and other pocket effects from the dresser.

Stepping out into the hall, I nearly ran into Kaleb who was, by the looks, about ready to knock on my door. His blue eyes widened in shock. I chuckled softly.

"Sorry, I didn't know you were out here," I offered as I pulled the door shut.

"I didn't mean to startle you. I was just going to stop by, as I had a few hours with nothing to do, and ask if you'd like a tour of the keep." He looked damn fine this morning. Maybe even sexier than he had yesterday, if that was even possible. The prince was working the corporate casual really well. Tweed vest over a white shirt, sleeves rolled up to expose nicely muscled forearms covered with gold hair, a russet tie that worked well with the blue tweed, and pressed jeans that hugged his thighs nicely. I loved the mash of denim on the lower half of a male body and a shirt, vest, and tie on the upper half. The man had style. That turned me right on.

"I'd love that. I can take some notes. Mind if we grab a bite first?" I enquired as my stomach rumbled. "I missed dinner, so could we maybe get breakfast."

He stepped aside to reveal a wheeled cart with several covered platters. "I thought I'd bring some breakfast, and we could eat on your patio."

I folded my arms over my chest. "How the hell did you wheel this all the way to my door, and me not hear it?"

"You had NBA YoungBoy turned up so loud, I doubt you would have heard a marching band strolling past your door." He gave me a lethal wink. Shit this man was sexy AF.

"Since you know who NBA YoungBoy is, I have to let that zinger go." With that, I flung my door back open, and we entered, the prince pushing the breakfast cart. He gave my clean room a quick glance, then wheeled the cart out onto the patio. Then, after I sat, the prince served me. Napkin lying over my slacks, he presented me with a platter heaped high with eggs, bacon, and fresh fruit. An urn of coffee and all the accoutrements sat steaming on the cart. Off in the distance, a honking sort of sound floated over the fjord.

"You got geese here?" I asked as I forked my food from the platter to my plate. Kaleb covered the eggs and meat back up, poured us both coffee, and took a seat across from me at the wrought iron table for two. The mountains and water and blue skies were hard to ignore, but the man across from me made them all pale in comparison. "We have Canada geese all over the place in Detroit. Damn things shit up all the parks. You can't swing a cat on Belle Isle and not hit a damn goose. They bite too."

He shook his head as he sipped his coffee. "No, that was a swan you heard. We have several pairs that nest here. And if you think geese are nasty, you should try bumbling up upon a swan with a sitting mate or cygnets. When we were kids, my father used to think it was hilarious when one of us would come racing back to the castle in tears after getting a firm pinch on the backside.

He and Mother always told us to leave the swans be, but of course we couldn't."

His face was soft now, his gaze reflective and slightly bittersweet. "I'm very sorry about your father."

"Thank you. That is most kind." He replied with the practiced tongue of a diplomat. "One never truly gets over losing a parent, even though we know, as adults, that they will most likely pass before we do."

"Yeah, as much as my father works my last nerve, I'm not sure what I'll do when he crosses the river Jordan."

"Yes, you and he work together. With an uncle too, correct?" His accent was polished and refined. My ears liked it. A lot. "That must be interesting at times. Working with my family has proven to be one of the most enjoyable and challenging aspects of my life."

I snorted into my sip of coffee. "Man, that was quite the statesmanlike way to say that. Generally, I just tell folks my family is a pain in my ass, but I love them anyway."

He laughed softly. "I do enjoy the way you speak. Right to the point."

"Yeah, you know us Americans. We threw all our manners into the Boston Harbor with that funky tea."

That made him roar. We spent the next hour on my patio, just talking. Well, maybe just talking didn't cover it properly. There were all kinds of long looks and vibing going on. The sexual tension was riding the cool air off the fjord, making me chilly and sweaty all at once.

"Perhaps we should get the tour underway. I have to go down into the capitol for business this evening." He rose gracefully. I put aside my cup and stood as well. "The staff will clean this up when they come in to tidy your room. Not that it needs much tidying. Shall we?"

I plucked my hat from the table, placed it on my head, and walked alongside the prince as we made our way down to the basement. I hesitated on the old, crumbly stone stairs, small notebook in hand, pencil artfully resting behind my ear.

"Is there a problem?" he asked. The man sounded so sincere. The cheeky shit knew my problem. "If you'd rather skip the basement, we can, but there are some issues down here that should have your knowledgeable eye cast upon them." I sniffed the air. They say you can smell ghosts. Something about candle wax or chimney smoke. All I could pick up was damp earth and Kaleb's fancy cologne. Even so, it paid to be careful. Dead folk were shifty. "If you'd like, I can hold your hand as we inspect the foundation."

I tore my gaze from the dimly lit steps leading into dead people land to stare at the prince. Man, he appeared to be earnest. Not a trace of taunting did I see. His gaze was really kind of warm. He offered me his hand.

"Not that I need to hold another man's hand to do a basement inspection. I'm simply unsure of the terrain and don't want to step in a puddle of dead folk goo with my new boots."

He nodded. "Of course. We'll be sure to avoid all goo, be it seeping fjord water or dead people ooze."

I slid my hand into his. His palm was warm and smooth, his grip strong. "Man, you had to mention dead people ooze." My fingers tightened around his, and he battled to keep a smile from breaking free. I respected that.

"We'll move along quickly."

He led me downward, talking steadily about this monarch or that castle. He pointed out quite a few cracks that were seeping water into the crypt. I took out my phone and started recording comments instead of trying to write out my thoughts. That way, I could still look professional and hold his hand. The place was spooky as shit. I would never get the need to keep dead Auntie Gert in the same place that sleeping took place. Everyone knows ghosts get into your head, then possess you when you're asleep. That shit is factual. Ask anyone.

Thankfully, the crypt was a quick pass through. We moved upstairs and left the corpses behind. Funny thing though. When we stepped out into the fresh air—at my request because I needed some damn sunshine on my face after that brush with the undead—Kaleb still held my hand. I didn't say anything at first because it was nice, and human contact was one sure way to drive away the shivers being that close to potential zombies had raised on my skin. We stood by the fjord for several minutes, talking—hand-in-hand—as the sun warmed us.

Eventually, we glanced at each other during a lull in the conversation. His eyes dropped to my lips, mine then flickered to his. The wind had shifted, and it blew up behind us, toying with his hair.

"Did you make a note about the pipes in the west corner of the royal crypt?" he asked. I shook my head, unable to tear my sight from his mouth. "Ah, then we should."

He reached for the pencil I had never used. The back of his fingers brushed my cheek. I exhaled roughly, the raspy sound reaching Kaleb as his pupils enlarged. His fingertips slid around my ear, the pencil forgotten, as he wet his lips and leaned in. I tipped my head, eager for the kiss.

Then, a fucking swan honked not ten feet from us. The call shot up my spine, scaring me half to death, and I yelped in fright. I may have yelled something about ghosts howling from the grave. Kaleb staggered back, his fingers slipping from my cheek and my grip.

We made a mad dash from the edge of the fjord, an irate looking white swan craning its long neck at us until we had enough distance from the water to appease him.

"Okay, that scared the living hell out of me," I panted, removing my hat to fan my face. Kaleb laughed nervously.

"Me as well." He coughed as we slowly made our way to the castle, my heart still thundering in my chest. We paused by the doors to the orangery. "Perhaps we can continue the tour later? Or I could call Harald to finish it with you? I really should have left an hour ago for the capitol."

"Sure, yeah, go do your princely duties. Harald and I will get the tour wrapped up. No worries."

He nodded, his sight lingering on me for a long moment. "It's been a wonderful morning, Marquis. I'll see you soon."

He offered me his hand again. This time, sadly, it was just for a handshake, a cool and detached handshake at that. He gave me a crisp little bow that I returned, and then, he was off, speeding around the side of the castle as if Satan were nipping at his heels. I stepped into the orangery, blew out a long breath, and called myself all kinds of an ass. We'd almost kissed. Right out in the open.

What the *hell* was going on with that? I was here on business. Dad would flay me alive if I fucked this up by letting my dick—which was all kinds of perky ATM—do the thinking. Again.

Shit. I adjusted my slowly flagging prick and went in search of Harald. If anyone could talk the lingering cravings for Kaleb from my blood, it would be Harald.

SIX

Kaleb

I WAS STILL RED-FACED OVER THE NEAR-KISS, THE NEXT morning, and had spent most of my finance meeting at the bank playing the scene over and over in my head. The *one* person I shouldn't be interested in, and I'd nearly given in and kissed him. I'd leaned in, touched his face, and even anticipated how the kiss might taste. I was all in for that freaking kiss. All I can think now is "thank goodness for the swans" because clearly they had more intelligence than I did.

Yes, Marquis was beautiful and funny, and the interest obviously goes both ways, but Mother had been right by warning me it was the most inappropriate thing I could do right now. Not that the other company representative had arrived, yet, to see me mess things up, but just from the written quotes, it was apparent that the other company had more to offer Norstoe regarding the cost and the timeline for deliverability.

It would be even more inappropriate to sleep with a supplier. Right?

Also, we only had a year until my mother's silver jubilee. We needed this castle to work for visiting dignitaries, family, friends, and the hordes of tourists descending upon the country. So, even though Marquis ticked all my boxes, I had to stay away from him.

"Okay, Your High—Kaleb, being brutally honest, you need to move the pump and the tanks down to the basement." He had his back to me, bending over and peering under our old water tank. I wasn't sure how long I could stand here because his slacks clung to his ass in such an obscenely beautiful way that I was about ready to burst out of my skin. I reached out to touch him, but he made a huff of disapproval about something he'd seen, and it snapped me out of staring and cut short my instinct to slide my hands down his spine and cup his ass.

He was still talking, but I'd zoned out. "... then we could move all the pipes that crisscross this building and have everything feeding from the new pumping system. I guess we're lucky the last refit in the thirties got rid of the lead." He straightened up, then patted the side of the tank and examined his fingers, rubbing them together and wincing. "You have a lot of dampness up here, and that can't be a good thing."

"It's always been wet up here, frosty in the winter." He frowned and to distract myself, I crouched and gestured under the tank at the nest of pipes that ran out from here and across the castle. "I used to play up here when I was little."

"You have an entire castle, all the grounds, a beautiful city, and your very own fjord, and you deliberately chose to spend time in a damp attic along with all these pipes?"

He was smiling, teasing me. I had to fight the need to tug him close and kiss the smile from his face.

God, I wanted to kiss him.

"Sometimes, when you want to set up a camp to escape the rest of your family, the best place to hide is where they least expect it."

I crossed the room, tapped the wall, waited until the sound was hollow, and then hunted around for something that I could use to pry open the old panel that had held telecoms equipment from way back. "I need something to…"

Marquis crowded me, not deliberately, but there wasn't much space in this far corner. He handed me a Swiss Army knife, and all I could focus on was that he was so close I could see the same need in his eyes as lived in me. We stared at each other for the longest time, the penknife was warm in my hand, and I forced myself back to the matter at hand.

"This is my hiding space," I explained, as it was better than facing the fact that lust consumed every part of me. I hadn't been up in the attic in the longest time, not since before I left for university, and I had no idea if the things I'd left inside would still be there. Was I really going to open this when there was a chance that everything I held as important was still there?

"What did you hide there? Is it lube and condoms?" He sounded hopeful as he leaned in toward the small door until we were only a breath apart. I fumbled with the penknife until I got a good grip on it, and, yanking myself away from staring, I used the blade to lever open the old door.

My box was still there.

I should have shut the door and pretended there was nothing, but Marquis reached in before I could do so.

"Is this treasure?"

"I guess so. At least it was when I left it behind as a dismissive eighteen-year-old on the brink of heading off to university and freedom."

"That's profound. I thought this would end up being your porn stash." He chuckled.

I let him pull the box out, then took it from him and placed it on the steady platform formed by some crossing pipes.

"I just need to remember the code for the padlock." Then, I moved the dial to the number that I thought it might be, but only reached the third before the padlock came apart in my hands.

"Told you this place was damp," Marquis noted. "It's rusted through."

I side-eyed him, and he smirked—the asshole.

Gently opening the lid, I could see that water had gotten inside the box, and what once had been a pristine collection of the best magazines ever, was now stuck together. It made me sad that part of my burgeoning sexual awakening was gone.

"I couldn't exactly access what I wanted on the castle network when nobody even knew I was gay until I was safely away in Scotland studying."

"Safely? What would have happened if you had told them before? Your mother and siblings don't seem like people who would judge you."

"They wouldn't. When I told my mom—over the

phone would you believe—she said she was sorry that I hadn't felt as if I could tell her before. But it wasn't some huge profound reason that I'd stayed quiet. It was the part of me that was private, and I only really shared it with Elsa."

Marquis chuckled, and the sound was like whiskey over ice. Why was it that everything he did was so hot?

"My parents said that I came out of the womb wearing a fancy hat and a sharp suit." Marquis leaned against the wall, seemingly not caring that it was damp and that his fancy designer jacket would get stained. "But yeah, the anxiety to conform here as a prince of Norstoe must have been intense. Hell, it must still be intense."

"We all have our tensions."

He nodded then, and I felt like he knew exactly what I was talking about, and he summarized it well.

"And this is where you hid all the parts of you that you never wanted anyone to see."

I closed my eyes briefly. "Yes and no, I was an asshole back then. I did what I wanted to do and fuck the consequences. You might not believe it, but it's only recently that I've taken responsibility seriously." Why was I telling him that? Was I that desperate for him to see me as responsible and in control that I had to spell it out for him?

"What you're saying is that if we'd met a few years back, we'd be fucking over the nearest pipe." Marquis was teasing, but the urge to grab him was strong.

"No. Yes… no."

He rolled his eyes, but he couldn't understand. I put family first—put Norstoe first—and I certainly didn't want to open the can of worms that was getting physical with Marquis.

He lowered his voice, sending tingles down my spine. "If this is where you keep your secrets, then maybe we could add one more?"

Without giving me a chance to answer, he cradled my face, held me still. There was no politeness or caution in the kiss. I opened my mouth to him and tasted as much as I could, gripping his jacket first, then sliding my hands down to rest on his ass. His cock was so damn hard against mine. I used to sit up in this place dreaming about sex, but the reality and the practicality of what we were doing were way beyond difficult. I couldn't get a proper hold of him because I had him squashed against the damp wall, and our kiss wasn't ending any time soon.

And just like that, Marquis ended the kiss, easing us apart, me chasing for more until I realized he'd stopped. Had I misread the situation? Was it me that started this kiss?

He must have seen all the confusion in my expression because he kissed my lips with nothing more than a butterfly touch.

"I want you so badly, but this isn't the right place to be doing this. If you want me as much as I want you, we should do this properly, with condoms, lube, and a bed. Or a chair. Anything that isn't a damp pump room."

Easing myself away from him, I grabbed the box of ruined magazines and held it to my chest. "No. That wouldn't be right... I have work to do, fireworks to organize. I need to go. This shouldn't have happened."

"It was always going to happen, Your Highness."

I left without looking back. I knew that if I spent a moment longer in the room with Marquis, I would be losing my mind and possibly handing over access to my heart. He didn't follow me, which was a good thing, and I made it back to my office without seeing anyone, which was another plus. I kept my head down, worked on my to-do list, and definitely did not keep touching my lips where I swear I could still feel his kiss.

After I finally managed to sign off on the fireworks, at the last minute for Eirik's birthday event, the sense of relief that at least one thing had gone my way today was overwhelming.

I felt as if I needed to celebrate, but it wasn't a nightcap, or an early night for worry-free sleep that I wanted. Not that I ever got entirely worry-free sleep, but that's another thing altogether. It was Marquis and the kiss that filled my thoughts, and what I really wanted to do was throw caution to the winds, go to his room, and see if the flirting could lead to more.

"What would you do?" I asked the second Prince Eirik's portrait, but he simply stared at me blankly.

"Why are you talking to a portrait?"

I spun to face Rune, who stumbled back at the energy in my reaction.

"Why are you sneaking up on people."

"I'm not," he said with a frown. "You're just jumpy. What's up?"

"I could ask you the same thing. I never see you around the castle now."

"I've been in my studio in the city," he murmured and couldn't quite meet my gaze. I saw he had a box with the flaps taped down, with a diaper brand on the outside.

"What's in the box?"

"Nothing."

"Nothing?"

"Charity stuff for uhm… charity." He was all kinds of shifty, but I also got the feeling he was about to run, and I wanted to talk to him, so I changed the subject away from the box.

"Will you be at Eirik's birthday party?"

"Of course." He looked affronted that I would ask. So much for changing the subject to a safe one.

"Look, Rune, we should talk about—"

"Later, little brother." He sidestepped me and scurried down the corridor before I could even finish.

I headed for my room, but Marquis was back in my thoughts. Maybe he was just the kind of man who casually flirted and never meant it to go further—maybe he was even trying to win me over for the bid—but unless I asked him, I would never know. I just needed to talk. It wasn't as if he would lunge at me the moment we were alone, instead I envisaged a sensible, measured discussion. With that in mind, I took a detour and headed toward Marquis's room.

To talk.

Walking down the corridor, I passed the chapel and the bust, recalling nearly every single flirty word Marquis and I had exchanged, and by the time I finally reached his door, I had convinced myself that talking was all we were going to do. I knocked and waited.

"Hello?" he said from inside.

"It's me, uhm, Kaleb." I didn't want to shout that too loud, knowing that the halls weren't empty, even this late —case in point, lurking brothers carrying boxes for charity.

"Come in."

The door wasn't locked, so with shoulders back, I pushed inside to see Marquis was propped up on his side in bed, reading.

How was it that even wrapped like a teddy bear in covers, I just had to see a glimpse of skin, and my libido went into overdrive?

It's just sex. Pull yourself together, have some mutual fun, scratch the itch, and then pretend it never happened.

"You have to understand this is just a one off. Okay?" I blurted, and he blinked at me in confusion.

"Huh?"

"Sex. With me."

"Oh."

It wasn't as if he was clambering out of bed and swooning, or getting his cock out and waving it around in celebration. Fuck, I misjudged this completely.

"I'm sorry. I'm disturbing you," I said after a moment and began to retreat.

"No, wait. Stay."

It was now or never. I shrugged off my jacket, letting it slip to the floor, and unbuttoned the top button of my shirt. He seemed to get exactly what I was doing, so he laid down his book, shoved some of the covers, and then extended his hand to me.

I was too weak to say no. I wanted this.

I wanted him.

SEVEN

Marquis

"YOU'RE NOT DISTURBING ME," I TOLD HIM, MY FINGERS meshing with his.

"I don't have much time before someone might need me..." He threw a leg over me, pinning me to the bed. Yeah, this was nice. As was the thick ridge of his erection gliding over my quickly hardening cock.

"At ten o'clock at night?"

"Princes never sleep," he reminded me, and I huffed.

"Well, I don't need much time." I grimaced. "That didn't sound good. You know what I meant. I can get you off real fast, baby."

His playful smirk disappeared as lust blossomed. The sun was low in the sky, slanting through the patio doors to warm his hair and face with butterscotch and pink. I wet my lips. I did love butterscotch.

He whispered something in Nordic, what it was I had no clue. He could have been calling on Odin's crows to come shit on my head for all I knew. I gripped his lean hips just as he fell forward, catching himself with locked arms, hands resting on either side of my head.

"Top or bottom?" His voice was thick like maple syrup on a cold day.

"Both." I slid my hands into his hair, enjoying the soft feel of it on my fingertips.

"Good, good, me too." His mouth crashed down on mine, his tongue skimming over my bottom lip. To hell with this slow hand stuff. He didn't have much time, and my dick was now totally in charge of Marquis. Not always a good thing. A whispered warning about trifling with the prince wafted around the inside of my skull. When his tongue met mine, that whisper blew right out of my ear and was gone. Maybe the swans would hear it. My hips rolled in time with his, cock scrubbing cock. Our tongues tangled and sparred, each of us giving and taking. He tasted of sweet coffee.

"Too many clothes," I huffed when we broke apart for air. His brow came to rest on mine as we fumbled between us to free our cocks. "Real nice prick, Kaleb."

I brought his mouth to mine, licking deep, stroking his tongue with mine as we both humped madly into his hand. I nipped at his lower lip, pulling on it with my teeth. He growled low and feral until I released it, then his lips crashed back over mine. I dug my nails into the nape of his neck while massaging his tight ass. His hips cracked like pistons as I blew apart, my cum coating Kaleb's hand. He grunted and tensed. Sweet, wet pulses of spunk made our grip slippery. We both jackhammered away like wild rabbits, milking each droplet from each other until his elbow buckled. My breath left my lungs in a rush, but still

I cradled his neck and ass, keeping him tight to me as we trembled and quaked.

It took me a minute to drift back from the stratosphere and form words.

"Are you okay?" I asked, then licked a stripe up his neck. He shivered, then nodded, his bearded cheek moving over my lips until his mouth found mine. This kiss was sweeter, less frenzied, but still as sensually sweet. I could kiss this man for hours.

"Yes, thank you." He slithered off me and onto the bed, rolling to his side as his thick lashes fluttered down to rest on his cheeks. "It's been a trying few weeks, and I needed that."

I sat up slowly, my body pliant, my head still a little fluffy from sex.

"Anything I can help with?" I glanced back at him, resting his head on his arm, his eyes shut, his cock still out. The urge to roll him to his back and gobble down his prick was strong.

"Nothing that need concern you." He heaved a mighty sigh and opened his eyes. His sight flittered to the open door, then moved languidly to me. "I know people assume that the life of a royal is all parties, yachts, and travel, but that is far from the truth."

"You forget dealing with old sea hags that want to steal your voice. Wait, that's a mermaid. Well, she was still a princess though, so the point is valid."

He snuffled in amusement, then reached for my arm. His touch set off tiny quakes that danced up to my shoulder and right to my extremities. The caress was tender. I liked it. A lot.

"You're funny. I've not smiled so much in… well, in far too long. Thank you for being so open and unimpressed with titles."

"Americans. Being unimpressed by titles since 1775."

His laugh bounced off the stone walls. My heart did this funky little twist and jive inside my chest. The man was intoxicating. And fun. And heartfelt. And sexy as motherfucking sin. "All kidding aside, if you need help just ask. I have some friends. We can do shit."

"Can you pull together a charity sporting event in less than two weeks?" He moved to his back, tucked his soft dick into his trousers, and zipped. Damn it. There went sucking his cock followed by riding him like a Norstoe stallion. Or him riding me. I was vers. It was all good.

"What kind of sport?" I rose, tucked, and zipped as well, then made my way to the bathroom.

"Well, it was supposed to be tennis, but everyone pulled out…" He drifted off as I turned the taps on to wash my hands. Even a plumber's son knew the faucet and fittings were ready to be made into new. They looked late seventies to me, and the water pressure in this old mound of rock was dismal to say the least.

"I can make a few calls to some friends. We could work up a charity hockey game for you. What's the goal and what's the organization we'd be playing to help?"

His heat appeared on my back. I startled, my sight flying from my soapy hands to a sated looking prince at my back. He leaned into me, arms going around me, to wet and lather his hands while his kiss-swollen lips moved up and down my throat. Stirrings were taking place in my boxer briefs. I might have pressed my ass back into his groin, just to let him know I would be down for a good dicking. Right here on the counter would work.

"Norstoe Children's Charity. But I can't ask you to—"

"I offered. Any charity for kids is a sure draw for hockey players."

"Oh. Do you know many hockey players?"

"Well, since I play forward for the Boston Rebels, yeah, I might know a few. Hundred."

"I thought you were a plumbing guy."

"Not really, just the pretty face of marketing."

"Hockey? I guess that explains why you're ripped."

"Sweet talker." Our fingers began to move and slide together, the scent of floral soap and his cologne doing funny things to my senses. As was the hot weight of him against my back. "Let me make some calls."

He kissed the shell of my ear, his whiskery chin tickling. "Thank you. I shouldn't ask favors from such a new acquaintance though."

I turned to face him, water running behind me, hands covered with white lather. "Kaleb, we just had our dicks in our hands and our tongues down each other's throats. I think we might be more than acquaintances. Friends with benefits? I'm leaving here in a few weeks so there's no way of anything more developing, but if you're down with sexing it up while I'm here?" I captured his face with my soapy hands and kissed the shit out of the man. When we came up for air, we were both hard again and breathing roughly. The man did things to me...

"I'm not sure that would be professional. But friends would be lovely."

A sadness crept over me that I really didn't want to delve into. I plastered on a smile and kissed him again.

"Pity, but I see what you're saying. This is a business trip. We don't want anyone to accuse you of playing favorites. Although do keep in mind that I can suck a cherry through a straw, so when the decision on the final plumbing company for the retrofitting is made…" I gave him a cheeky wink that made him chuckle. I liked the sound of his laughter.

"Friends it will be then. Thank you for this little diversion. It helped a great deal. I'll see you at breakfast?"

Diversion? I nodded, watching in fascination as the Kaleb that had come to me in desperate need of simply being Kaleb was now replaced with the cool royal personage of Prince Kaleb.

"Sure, yep, see you at breakfast." I kissed his cheek. We dried our hands, and he took a minute to fix himself up before leaving my room with a short, courtly bow and a tender smile.

After the door clicked shut, I stripped down to my underwear, set the alarm for seven on my phone so I didn't miss breakfast with the sexy prince, and then sat on the bed, confused, tired, and hungry. Sighing heavily, I crawled under the duvet that smelled of Kaleb and closed my eyes to ponder on how I would handle the next few weeks. Focus on the plumbing and the charity hockey game. Then fly home and return to the life of Marquis Miller. Yep, that was the plan. No more sex. It was a good plan.

Shame it felt like a shitty plan.

Swimming through the fog of a dead sleep, I came around to the sound of polite, but sharp rapping on my door as Gunna played on my phone.

"Don't care how dead you are, that's not a trump suit if it's missing a king," I mumbled as I worked to wipe away the vestiges of a weird ass dream starring me, several dead monarchs, and a game of spades clinging to my consciousness. The knocking grew more insistent. Yawning widely, I stretched and squinted at the sun flowing into my room. Damn, this place was weird. The sun got brighter as the day went on. I'd never noticed that when I'd been in the UK or France. "Yeah, come in!" I shouted, then scrubbed at my face with the duvet. I caught a whiff of sex on the coverlet that took me right back to the short, but sizzling, time with Kaleb. Did I dream that as well?

Someone knocked on the door again, and I wriggled up, hoping it would be the sexy prince, but instead, a dude in a black suit opened the door at my *come in*. He was a small guy, youngish, with a mop of red hair and a wary smile.

"I'm Geoffrey, Mr. Miller. Apologies for the intrusion, but I thought you might need something."

"Something? Like…"

"Uhm…" he stared at his feet, and then, cleared his throat. "Harald was concerned you'd taken ill, as it's quite late…"

"Late?"

"It's well past noon, sir."

I blinked like a dullard. "Noon?" Man, the jet lag was still monkeying with my inner clock. Or maybe it was the sex I'd had. "Wait. Did I sleep through breakfast?" I grabbed my phone. Yep, it was well past noon. Damn it. I knew I should have set the alarm to the miserable ass beeping, instead of my rap caviar playlist. Kodak Black was now on about super gremlins. Had I blown my only chance to see Kaleb today? Would he be cool, or would there be a crackling undercurrent between us? My dick began to perk up. Yep, there would be an undercurrent. At least on my end.

I got dressed in a rush, pulling on some white jeans, a white tee, and a soft gray cardigan. After, I put my feet in some tasteful gray and white Backman and Taylor gray suede sneakers with no socks. I shoved my phone into the back pocket of my pants, as well as my wallet. Out the door I went, stomach growling like a lion, to find the corridor empty. I paused, looked left and then right, and set off to the left. I made a few turns, looked out a window to see the swans on the fjord, and then climbed down a short flight of stairs that did not look like the stairs I'd followed Kaleb up yesterday.

This is what happens when you pay no mind to where you're going and focus on someone's ass.

Fuck off. That ass is worth getting turned around.

The stairs ended. Like just ended. At a stone wall. Oh-kay. I climbed back up and went down another hall with tapestries. Where did they get all the wall hangings from? Was that a big business in Europe? Shop Tapestries 'R Us! Your all-in-one tapestry shopping destination!

After fifteen minutes of aimless wandering, I found

myself outside in some sort of courtyard. A brisk breeze coming off the fjord was cool on my face. The air was rich with the sound of horses, and clean, aside from the horses' stench. I paraded around an old stone arch, the sun bright on my head. Voices and laughter rang out. A massive stable sat on a small rise ahead of me, a dirt lane lined with lush maples, green leaves blowing in the wind. Bewitched by the beauty of the sight, I ambled down the lane, fingers skimming the mossy rocks on the low stone wall that ran along the winding road. It was a majestic scene with the mountains in the far distance.

It became even more beautiful when Kaleb and a young woman came thundering down the lane on dark brown horses. I jumped back to clear the way just as the riders—both in their fancy riding habits—saw me and brought their beasts to a sudden halt, front hooves kicking up bits of sod, dirt, and pebbles. I thought the bugger had looked good in bed, but seeing him now astride a massive horse, with those tight riding pants hugging his thick thighs, his blond hair flowing out from under his helmet, and his cheeks flush, made my cock incredibly happy.

Kaleb slid off the horse, his blue eyes wide with worry, and rushed to me.

"Are you okay?!" He took my hand between his as he looked me over.

"Yeah, I'm fine. Totally good. I was just… well, I kind of got lost in the castle. I slept through breakfast, and this Geoffrey guy woke me up, and I decided to explore, only this place is enormous. I'm doing the bread crumb thing next time I leave my room." I realized I was rambling, which was not something I normally did. Also, I noted that the young miss on the dark brown horse was eyeing me with intense interest. Or maybe it was the way Kaleb was holding my hand as he smiled at me that had her attention. "Yeah, so here I am. Nice stable. Pretty horses. That your girlfriend?"

Kaleb laughed riotously as did the petite, pretty blonde.

"God no. I'm his sister, Princess Elsa. It's a pleasure to meet you, Mr. Miller." Now that I looked, I could see the familial resemblance. Her not having a beard threw me off. "Kaleb has chattered on about you endlessly this morning." I looked at Kaleb and sort of got lost in those sapphire depths of his. "Okay, well, I'm going to finish my ride. Why don't you escort Mr. Miller to the kitchen and see if Magda can find a little something for him?" A moment passed. "Kaleb?"

Kaleb jolted as if someone had hooked a jumper cable to his balls. He dropped my hand, blushed furiously, and then said something to his sister that made her nod and giggle. My cheeks were a bit warm as well, when the prince, his horse, and I made our way to the courtyard.

"I'm sorry for galloping up on you like that. Do you ride?"

I threw him a look that made the pink in his cheeks turn to crimson. "Ah, right, we discussed riding already. Ahem, well, this is the back door to the kitchen." He motioned to a door surrounded by ivy. "I'd venture inside, but I smell of horse and my boots are filthy. Magda, she's the head cook, would come after me with a broom if I dared to enter her kitchen after coming from the stables."

His horse nickered behind him. "I'll peek inside and

see if I can find Magda then. You better keep yourself out here."

The corners of his mouth curled up. "Indeed. I'll text Harald and have him meet you in the kitchen in, say, half an hour?" I nodded. "Perfect. Until dinner then." He bowed, then turned on his heel, leading his horse away from the door before this formidable Magda found horse shit on her stoop. I watched him walking away, my gaze riveted to his thighs before he climbed up on his horse and trotted off, head high like a real-life Prince Charming.

Suddenly, traveling across the world to talk plumbing up a mossy old castle didn't seem so bad.

EIGHT

Kaleb

"WHAT WAS THAT?" ELSA WHISPERED, THEN POKED AT MY chest.

"What was what?" I had debated ignoring the question because I wasn't joking when I said I needed a shower and stat. The idea of being trapped on the back steps to our quarters with a sister who is far too perceptive for her own good—something she's inherited from Mother—was horrific.

"You know what." I attempted to open the door, but she slid under my arms and leaned against it, staring at me, waiting for an answer. It could have gone one of three ways: I say nothing, tell her the truth, or attempt to come up with a lie that was good enough to cut the conversation dead. "Tell me everything."

"There's nothing to tell you."

"Oh my God," she lowered her voice, "you fucked the gorgeous builder guy."

"Plumber. Well, not plumbing; he's actually a hockey player and a plumber. A plumbing hockey player—"

"He's not been here long, and you already... wow you're good." She fake-swooned.

"And it took you how long to get married to Vincent?" I was aiming for sarcasm, which normally took her attention from whatever she was trying to tease me about, but she got a familiar sly expression, and I knew I'd started something that wasn't going to stop.

Her eyes widened, and she pressed a hand to her chest. "Wait what? You want to marry him this quickly?"

"What? No. You did that. Not me, it was just a fuck and..."

She blinked at me innocently as I realized what I'd admitted. "Uh-huh."

Damn her ability to read me like an open book.

"Don't tell anyone," I warned, and she gave me one last poke.

"Slut," she deadpanned. "And what do you mean, he's a hockey player?"

I pulled out my cell and thumbed to the page I'd bookmarked. The team's Instagram is dedicated to all things Boston Rebels, including some rather fine photos of Marquis Miller. She peered at the photos, and then snatched my phone and scrolled.

"Oh my," she exclaimed and fanned her face. "Do you see how good he looks in uniform?" She tapped the screen. "Like, like..."

"Stop that!"

"No one will know who you are Mr. Anonymous John underscore Smith dot 87 dot g something or other, whatever that means. Like. Like." I reached for the phone, but she pirouetted away—damn her ballet training. Then she stopped, and her mouth fell open. "Did you see the one with the hockey stick and the teddy bear—"

"Yes."

"And the one where he's wiping his face with his shirt and the abs are right there…"

"Yep."

"Oh, wait, he has a sexy friend. Well, more than one, actually. Oh, he's nice." She tilted the phone. "Moral Dunkirk, well, he's a big Viking if I ever saw one, all that red hair, and he's big. They're all big. Oh wait, is that your Marquis again…" She pinched the photo to enlarge it. "He's… oh my God… those pants leave nothing to the imagination, and he has one fine—"

"He's not my Marquis." I snatched my phone back before she could move, and she pouted. Growing up, we'd always shared photos of the sexiest men, but there was something about Marquis that I wanted to keep for myself, even if it was just a one-off hookup.

"Why no sharing of the sexy hockey player?" She quirked an eyebrow in question.

"Why no sharing of the wedding in Vegas?" I could have given too much away in my defense of the photos, but Marquis had a Kaleb-shaped stamp on him, and he wasn't a piece of meat.

Even though I fucked him and left.

"Touché, little brother, touché."

"Only by three minutes." I rolled my eyes, and she went on tiptoes to kiss my cheek and gathered me into a hug. The whole reason we'd gone for a ride was the fallout from the marriage press release was brutal, and she didn't want to be anywhere near the palace right now.

Particularly given Vincent had disappeared, although not in a sinister way; he'd be back soon. He was being briefed, which was Harald-speak for delivering a speech about procedure, and the poor guy had a ton of royal protocols he had to know to be Elsa's husband. I hoped he wouldn't run screaming in the opposite direction.

"Have you forgiven me yet for marrying Vincent without telling you?" she asked in a whisper against my ear, and I held her close.

"There's nothing to forgive as long as you're happy."

"I am. I know that it isn't fair to dump it all on you, but I'm only teasing about Marquis. I guess he'll be there tonight? Mother and Harald want the big entrance from Vincent all suited and booted, with me on his arm, but I'd rather we were able to slip in the back. Anyway, I want to meet Marquis, and I promise not to mention the slutty sex, and you know I love you, right?"

That was a lot to digest. "Of course, I do, and I love you too. I never want you to think you can't talk to me, only next time you get married, can you give me a heads up." She pulled back a little and stared up at me, and there was a twinkle in her eye.

"Sure," she responded, and then she went left to go to her new quarters, and I headed right to go to mine. I hadn't been joking when I said I needed a shower, and the sooner the better. I stripped as soon as I was inside the door, consigning my clothes to the laundry and heading for the bathroom. The shower wasn't in the best state of repair—the family rooms were last on the list to be fixed—but the hot water was plentiful. As soon as it hit my back, I began to relax. Sometimes, the only peace I got was being on a horse or in a shower, but that was part of the job I was born into, and one I loved. No one asked me to take on the duty of repairing the castle; no one asked me to organize royal events; no one ever told me I had to do anything.

But I still did it.

Making amends was what Eirik called it after one particularly long day when he found me in my study still working on castle plans. He'd suggested I was making up for the years of enjoying my freedom, but then, he looked at being the heir to the throne as a kind of prison sentence, whereas I didn't see my family as a jail of any kind.

I washed from head to toe, the water steady on my back, hot enough to pinken my skin. And while the scent of lemons filled my bathroom, I relaxed and unbidden memories of what I'd done with Marquis filled my thoughts. I blame the fact I haven't had sex in months and the pressure of everything, ignoring the little voice that told me I was no better than the stupid college kid who'd slept with anything that moved and fed right into the playboy prince name. It was absolutely the worst thing I could have done, when I should have stayed impartial and fair and not slept with the one man who I was supposed to be dealing with on a business level.

But the reminder of him lying on the white sheets, sprawled and needy, and his body... I gripped my cock, which was way too interested in focusing on Marquis—anything to stop myself from getting off in the shower to those memories. Only my hand moved. I swear I didn't mean it to, but the feeling of my slippery hand on my hard cock and the image of Marquis pushing against me was enough to have me reaching for the tile to stay standing. I could imagine Marquis in here with me, on his knees, water running over his skin, his gaze fixed on me, and his mouth stretched around my cock.

Fuck. With just the thought of that, I was coming so hard it was as if I hadn't had sex for freaking years. I watched the evidence swirl down the drain, then shut off the shower and wrapped my stupid self in a towel and slumped to my bed.

Someone knocked on my door, and I had images of Harald with some issue that needed my attention, or was it Marquis? My dick tried to raise with a valiant effort, but I pushed my towel down and willed it away.

"It's me," Eirik shouted from outside. My big brother never did anything quietly, and I sighed.

"I'm getting dressed!" I shouted back, but that didn't deter him, and he let himself inside just as I was pulling on underwear.

"We need to talk!" Eirik announced, and I ignored him long enough to get my pants on, but he wasn't waiting. "Did you fuck the contractor?"

I paused just as I was buttoning my crisp white shirt, but didn't give him the satisfaction of confirming a goddamn thing. This castle might not just have physical holes, but it was leaky as hell with gossip, although I could guess who told him, and when I tracked my sister down, she'd be in so much trouble.

"Kaleb, answer me."

I turned to face the future king, who was clearly out of sorts this morning. His usual smart appearance was all rumpled, and there was blood on his shirt, not to mention a bruise on his cheekbone.

"Have you been in a fight?" I countered.

"Don't change the subject." Eirik threaded his fingers through his dark hair, and it stood on end for a short time before falling into messy layers. "Elsa told me you fucked the contractor!"

Just as I thought. No doubt she'd been changing the subject over the wedding issue, but twin secrets were a thing. "I'm guessing that was to get you off the subject of talking about Vincent."

"Why was the Vincent thing a secret—why was I the last to know? How can I be king one day, if no one tells me anything? I don't know what in hell's name is going on half the time. One sibling married, the other one paying off crooks, and you sleeping around with random contractors."

Paying off crooks? By process of elimination, it had to be Rune. "Eirik—"

"You need to sleep with the other contractor when she gets here."

I gripped his arms, and he winced. "There are two fatal flaws in your plan. One, she's a woman, and two, I'm gay."

Eirik blinked at me. "So?"

"Okay, let me explain the gay to you."

"Fuck you, Kaleb." He pulled out of my hold and yanked at his hair again. "I know you're gay, but you've wrecked everything, and Elsa has wrecked everything, and Rune is a bastard who needs…"

"Why did Rune have to pay off crooks?"

"I didn't say that." He flat out lied because surely he'd implied it. He rambled on about propriety, and I tuned him out and pulled on a light jacket before checking my appearance in the mirror. I should have shaved, but I was clearly way too happy rubbing one off in the bathroom to think about that. Never mind, I wasn't seeing anyone until the party later, so I could get away with not shaving. Which reminded me, I never officially invited Marquis to Eirik's birthday celebrations, and I really should do that. I could try to find him and invite him while he sucked my cock.

"… when were you going to explain that one!"

I realized Eirik was still talking, and I had to focus back on the matter at hand and not on the fact I wanted Marquis on his knees for me in a shower. Or out of a shower—I was shower-flexible.

"Sorry?" I turned to face him, and I swear the bruise on his face was getting worse. "Why was Rune paying off crooks, and what happened to your face, Eirik?"

"Don't change the subject."

"Too late, it's changed."

"Rune was drunk is all, and I was helping him get undressed, but he shoved me away, and I, um… hit the closet door… it's embarrassing as fuck."

I ignored the fact that Eirik had muttered that Rune had punched him. "Rune was drunk? When? Now?"

"Last night, he was all over the place on hundred-year-old whiskey, not sure what's going on with him, kept talking about raspberry yogurt."

I scrubbed at my face. Me sleeping with a contractor or not sleeping, as the case may be, was a hell of a long way down the list.

"I can't do this." Eirik slumped to the chair by the

door, right on top of the folder of paperwork I'd been checking through when I was in bed last night.

"Do what?" I asked carefully.

"Go to my own party with this." He pointed at his face, and I breathed a sigh of relief that it was something simple that I could deal with.

"Go to the kitchen for ice, tell Harald, and he'll do something to fix it." I waved, then, to indicate whatever clever thing Harald would do. "You can go now. I have places to go and people to see."

"The contractor?"

"No." *Yes.*

"So, Elsa says you plumbed new depths with the contractor rep." He sighed at his own joke. "What exactly were you thinking?"

"Thinking didn't come into it." I'd had enough of the conversation because I knew exactly where it would be leading. With holier than thou Eirik of the bruised face, pronouncing that I was letting the family down when it was him, the future king of freaking Norstoe, who looked as if he'd gone ten rounds in a boxing ring.

"Not changing the subject at all, but Mother added Antoni to the invite list, and he's arriving in a couple of hours, and Mother said that you and he were—"

"Out," I ordered, not wanting to talk about Prince Antoni, gesturing that Eirik get the hell out of my room with haste. As soon as he stepped outside, I followed him and shut the door behind us. Before Eirik could even go there with Mother's matchmaking efforts between me and Antoni, I jogged away and lost him in the maze of corridors that was the back way to the kitchen. I didn't know if Marquis would still be there, but I was never happier than to see him sitting at the huge wooden table, nursing a coffee and chatting away with Magda.

She stood as soon as she saw me and said: "Morning, Your Highness."

"Morning, Magda." I waved for her to sit down, but she pointed behind herself at something that must have been important because she curtsied and left.

"Does that get annoying?" Marquis asked as I slid into the chair she'd just abandoned.

"What?" I eyed his coffee and wondered if I should have gotten coffee before I sat down, only to have one placed next to my hand. I glanced up at a smiling Magda. "You're a lifesaver, thank you." She hustled off, and I focused on Marquis. "What was the question again?"

"The curtsying and bowing." Marquis made this elaborate bow, which was cute given he was sitting down, and I sipped my coffee slowly. "Do you find it annoying?"

"I don't have much say in it," I said and glanced back to see Magda in the far kitchen. "It's not that I like or dislike it, just that I've gotten used to it, and I always try to return the respect."

He nodded as if he'd seen that. "I guess it's like the kids who get all tongue-tied when they meet a player on the team. It always feels weird that they hero worship one of us, and we take that responsibility seriously." He leaned into me and lowered his tone. "Any chance of more of what happened before?" I know he was being circumspect, but I really had to cut this off before it had a chance to be more.

"Regretfully, no."

He shrugged and sat back in his chair, resting his mug against his chest and sighing. "Shame."

"But I did want to track you down and invite you to a formal dinner this evening, for my brother's birthday. It's not a big event, not official, but there will be fireworks after and a small parade before."

He huffed a laugh. "Nothing too big then, just fireworks and a parade," he deadpanned, then grinned widely. "Good thing I packed my best suit," he leaned in again, "it's kind of tight around the ass, and if I get hard, boy it's an eyeful."

He left me, taking his coffee, then chatting briefly to Magda, gifting her with one of his perfect smiles before sauntering away as if he hadn't just handed me a plate full of sexy to juggle.

Goddammit, just a few words from him, and I was hard enough to pound nails, and probably stuck in this chair for the foreseeable future.

Typical.

NINE

Marquis

PRINCES WERE JERKS.

I take that back. Not all princes were jerks. The rock star Prince had been, and would forever be, a god. May we take a moment to worship his purple high-heeled boots, knowledge of how to apply liner, and otherworldly musical talent. Amen. We will now pass a raspberry beret for contributions.

Other than Mr. The Artist, all other princes were jerks. Especially the prince who was currently hobnobbing with Kaleb. I glanced down the table filled with royalty, and friends of royalty, to find Kaleb and the prince—a royal douche called Antoni—who was currently salivating over Kaleb, engrossed in conversation.

Princes Kaleb and Antoni made a striking couple, which made me even more pissed off. Kaleb with his golden hair and beard, and Antoni with his shiny black locks and piercing blue eyes. Both were lean, tall, White, handsome, regal, and sexy as shit. And here I sat, the boy from the Motor City, the only dark-skinned person at the forty-foot-long table where the princes looked like they belonged together. That made the seafood chowder that I'd eaten sit badly.

Kaleb threw back his head and laughed at something Antoni said. I sawed into my rare roast beef as if it needed to be killed again, stewing at the jealousy bubbling in my chest, then cussing myself out for being jealous. I'd known Kaleb for what? Two days? We'd had one brief second together, and then, he had slammed down the moat on anything else. Did you slam down a moat? No, that was the water thing around a castle. You raised the bridge over the moat and slammed the big wooden door. Right. Well, upped the bridge and shut the door in my face in terms of future hookups, which was totally the correct thing to do. We were here on business.

"The beef is a little rare for my taste."

I glanced to the left to smile at Alexandria Wells, the other plumbing representative. She was a stunning woman with long brunette hair, green eyes, and legs that went on for miles. Also, her breasts were quite plump and tastefully on display in her sleek silver cocktail dress. She was a little too touchy-feely for my liking, but I could play the game of schmoozing if I had to. There was something about her that was a little... off. I blamed my dad for filling my head with nonsense about her family's reputation.

"Mine too," I replied as I lowered my fork and knife. "I grew up with a father who charred the living hell out of anything on the grill."

"Your father sounds like mine," she said with a smile, and this time, it was genuine. "Every cookout we ever had, the burgers were like hockey pucks. Speaking of hockey, your Rebels did quite well last season. Making it to the playoffs was quite the feat with so many skilled teams in the Atlantic. I'm originally from Toronto, so my heart will always be with my home team, but your season was really impressive."

"A beautiful woman who likes hockey. Will you marry me?"

Her laugh was light and airy. And, it seemed, traveled, for Kaleb glanced our way from the other end of the table. His slim brows knotted. I smiled sweetly and turned all my attention to Alexandria. Why give me that look when he was the one who'd been flirting with Antoni-His-Royal-Studliness all evening?

"Toronto is rebuilding. Give them a few years, and they'll be real contenders," I said.

"All we need is some good defensemen to give our goalie some protection. There are far too many shots on goal reaching him."

And just like that, the meal became far more enjoyable. A whole hour passed with course after course of excellent food, fine wine, a birthday cake that was as big as a VW van, and a charming dinner companion on either side. Princess Elsa watched me and her twin intently. Her husband Vincent, the former-bodyguard-now-duke, according to the kitchen gossip I couldn't have failed to hear, looked as out of place as I felt.

The queen made a toast to the crown prince. We all cheered, and then the meal came to an end. Thank all the Nordic gods. Light chit-chat took place as the guests milled around a large den with brandy in hand. Alexandria and I talked for a bit longer, then she excused herself and went to bed, citing jet lag. I kissed her hand, and bid her adieu and sweet dreams. I could be courtly, too.

I wandered outside after dinner, sneaking around the castle and getting utterly lost, until a kindhearted maid pointed me in the direction of the orangery. The room was warm with the residual heat of a sunny day. I shrugged out of my gray suit jacket, undid my tie, and walked among the potted trees, tables, smaller ferns, and greenery, breathing in the moist air, then peeking skyward to view a million stars through the curved glass roof. My dress shoes made soft sharp sounds on the tile floor. The air was thick with the smell of rich peat, dirt, and flowers coming into bloom. I paused by a spikey plant heavy with dark violet flowers.

"That's a red *Leucadendron Proteas*." My head snapped to the left as Kaleb walked closer on silent feet. "They're endemic to South Africa. Mother loves them."

"So, you're a botanist too?" I folded my arms over my chest, my coat draped over my forearms, my tie in my back pocket. "Where's the other prince?"

"Which one? There are several milling around the castle."

"The one that you were so chatty with all night." I winced at how churlish that sounded. "Tall guy, black hair, cheekbones you can set a coffee mug on."

"Antoni? I'm not sure. Perhaps he and your giggly competitor are off somewhere discussing flapper valves." He took a few steps closer, breaking the moonlight flowing into the sunroom.

I held my ground as my skin began to prickle with his

proximity. "Maybe they are. I don't know where she went after we had a long talk about ballcocks."

His last step brought him chest to chest with me. I lowered my arms to see if he would close those extra few inches. My cock was stiff and leaking already.

"Oh, so it was ballcocks you were discussing?" His breath wafted over my face. I breathed it in, savoring the rich smell of good brandy. "Should you be spending so much time with someone who is trying to underbid you? Did you offer to show her your wares?"

"Gentlemen don't talk plumbing, then tell. What about Prince Studly? What did you two talk about that had you so entertained?" I chucked my coat to a nearby white wrought iron table, then shoved my fingers into that gold hair that I'd been dreaming about touching throughout that boring ass dinner.

"The upcoming Trooping of Color ceremony for his father's birthday, investitures, the recent global warming conference in Geneva that we both attended, and a new polo pony that he's thinking of buying."

I tightened my fingers in his hair. He stepped in closer still, his body now flush to mine, the fat ridge of his hard prick pressing into my groin.

"Fuck that is some sexy talk."

"I couldn't focus on what he was saying because all I could do was watch you and that plumbing woman tee-heeing and rubbing knees under the table."

I ghosted a kiss over his lips. He shuddered. My cock throbbed. "Jealous?"

"That would be foolish, since we're not doing this again." His hands settled on my hips, moving me slightly to the left to bump dicks. A low growl escaped me at the contact, so I led his mouth to mine, claiming it, devouring it. His hands moved to my ass, fingers biting into my cheeks, his tongue sparring with mine as he steered me to a wall. My back slammed into the thick glass as I held his mouth to mine. "Shit, you make me mad with want."

"You fucking me or am I fucking you?" I asked, then licked a stripe along his jaw.

His reply was to spin me around to face the fjord. I nearly came right then, splaying my fingers on the cool glass as he reached around me to undo my slacks while he feasted on my neck. My brow met the glass with a thunk at the same time my slacks slid down my legs to puddle around my ankles.

"Sitting so far away from you, while you were making eyes at that plumbing woman, was torture," he confessed, his words hot puffs on the back of my neck, his zipper going down with a sharp sound that made me weak in the knees. I loved a good fucking as much as I loved fucking someone. I pushed my ass back, my breath fogging the glass as the moon glowed silver-white on the dark waters of the fjord.

"Sitting so far away from you while you were making giggles with Antoni was torture," I parroted, taking my prick in hand. "I have condoms and lube in my wallet."

His slick, latex-covered cock at my hole stole my breath.

"As do I," he panted, taking a nip of my neck as he eased two slippery fingers into me. My moan rolled off the glass wall. I spread my legs as far as I could, then closed my eyes, letting him work me open with greedy, strong plunges.

"Shit, that's... UNGH." He brushed my prostate, taking all the oxygen from the room. "Fuck me. I'm too close."

Running my palm over the wet head of my prick, I shivered in delight when he replaced his fingers with that magnificent cock of his.

"I'll go slow," he whispered. I pushed my hips back with a snap, taking all of him in one thrust that wrung a yelp of pleasure from me. He grunted in surprise. "Okay, so not slow then."

"Not slow. Fast, hard... before someone takes... oh fuck! A walk by the... harder. Give it to me!"

Hands pressed against the glass, I begged for more, and Kaleb gave it to me. Pounding into me so fiercely that my brow bounced off the glass several times. Talk about fucking amazing. I'd never suffered a brain injury from sex. All the concussions I'd ever had were never this much fun to get. I worked my cock in time with each slapping thrust. "It's right there... fuck me harder. Roll your hips. Oh, fuck yeah, Kaleb!" I roared as his prick found the sweet spot. Cum flew out of me, hitting the window in pearly ropes. My body clenched around him.

Breathless and limp as a towel, I clung to the wall, fingertips squealing as he rose to his toes for that last push that propelled me heavenward. Body locked, his cock kicking inside me, my body pumped more spunk over my hand. He rolled his hips a few times, making me tremble and beg for more even though there was no way I could take more. He was so deep...

"Oh God," he panted, his forehead coming to rest on the back of my head. "Oh God above that was… incredible." He nibbled at my neck, sending shivers all the way down to my toes as I drifted like a dandelion blown on the sweet rush of the most amazing fuck I've ever had.

I turned my head a bit, and he found my lips. The kiss was awkward, sloppy, and devastating. I whimpered when he pulled out, his hand lingering on my hip to guide me around to face him. He was a sight in the moonlight. Pupils blown, cheeks flushed, mouth moving closer. I shoved my hands into his hair, sealing his mouth to mine. My bare ass met the glass and that made me gasp. The kiss ended, but I held fast to his hair, keeping his nose tight to mine as I tried to read what was in those pretty eyes of his.

"So glad to see that we didn't have sex again," he whispered, then chuckled.

"Yeah, me too. When can we not have sex again?"

He stole a light kiss. "If your competitor finds out, that will be it for Miller & Miller. You'll have to withdraw your bid, as our being involved in an intimate relationship would taint any kind of fair and equitable decision that I might make."

"Then we don't let anyone find out." I kissed him hard. He nodded, his lips wandering over my cheeks and eyes until he found my lips yet again.

"My sister and brother already know."

"Will they say anything?" I played with his hair, which was a little bit sticky now.

"No, I've got too much on them, but it could look bad if—" I cut him off with another kiss. Then another. Then another. "They won't say anything. Can I come to your room later?"

"If you do, I'm going to fuck you into another time zone. Just warning you."

He smiled seductively, and damn, if my dick didn't twitch. This man was sin personified, and I was truly a weak, weak sinner.

"I'll be there in an hour. I need to shower."

"No point to shower yet." I tasted his mouth once more. "Just bring more condoms, lube, and a leather strap to bite down on."

"God above."

Yeah, I didn't think the big sky guy was going to want to be watching what was going to take place between the prince and me over the next few weeks. We might end up smote, and that wasn't on my bucket list of fun things to do with a sexy royal in a Scandinavian country.

TEN

Kaleb

AFTER TEN DAYS OF DELIBERATION, OUR CHOICE WAS simple, and in a way, I was glad about it. The quote from Alexandria Wells was not only lower overall, but the company assured us they could deliver much quicker than Miller & Miller. This meant that I didn't have to worry about how my sleeping with Marquis might affect my decision. I just hoped Marquis didn't think that I'd handed it to the other company because he'd warmed my bed and I was deliberately going in the opposite direction.

Still, I'd come to a general conclusion in my own mind that I was now using as an excuse to get Rune into my study. I'd told him I wanted him to sign off on the contract, and he'd grumbled, but at least he'd shown up. He looked as if he hadn't slept in a week, and he peered at me over the top of his glasses.

"You know that the decision is on you. I don't get why you need me to get involved," he grumbled again, yawned widely, and rubbed at the dark circles under his eyes. I knew my brother sometimes got lost in his art and wouldn't sleep, and I worried about him.

"Just read the paperwork, Rune, and give me your opinion, okay?"

Rune slumped down in his chair, gripping the papers, and glancing at each page, but I could tell he wasn't reading what was on there. I wasn't the only one who'd noticed how exhausted he was. Mother had cornered me at dinner and voiced her concerns about him. She would never come out and ask me to get to the bottom of it, but after patting my arm and looking worried, I knew I'd be digging. Not to mention finding out why he'd gotten drunk, and how it connected to Eirik's face meeting a door.

Getting Rune here in the study was just a step in the right direction, and after he read the final page, he reached for a pen.

"What do you think about the ghost clause on page eight? Does it concern you?" I asked in all seriousness.

He glanced up at me and blinked as if he'd only just realized where he was. "Huh?"

"Page eight, provision for ghost manifestation."

"I didn't…" He shakily placed the papers on my desk. "Shit, Kaleb, I wasn't even reading it."

"I know."

He blinked at me as if he needed to try hard to re-focus, then he cleared his throat. "For real, someone wants a ghost clause?"

"No, someone doesn't want a ghost clause, idiot."

"Don't call me an idiot!" he snapped.

"Then don't fall for my shit," I teased.

He blinked at me for a few seconds, then tears

collected in his eyes as he hunched in on himself and folded himself like a piece of paper, crossing his arms over his chest and hugging himself tight.

"Rune?" I moved around the desk immediately. "Shit, what's wrong? I was teasing, I didn't mean to…"

I took him into an awkward hug, and he briefly clung to me, then eased away.

"Shit," he muttered and swiped at his face before straightening. "I'm okay."

He was far from okay, but Rune was the kind of man who held all his emotions inside—even as kids, he was the last one to cry. I knew him well enough that me poking at whatever was going on wasn't going to help. The last time I'd seen him as pale and needy as this, he'd been on the sharp end of being bullied at prep school. Eirik had fixed that shit, but not before Rune had struggled without telling us for way too long.

"Does this have to do with the fight with Eirik?"

He startled, and then stared at me. "I don't know what you mean."

"Eirik said you got drunk, and then, got into a fight."

"No, we didn't fight. He was helping me, and he fell into a door." He pulled himself upright. "Is he telling you we had a fight?"

I ignored the question. "Why were you getting drunk? Is everything okay?"

He went even paler. "It's nothing that has anything to do with you." He wasn't aggressive with his words, if anything, he sounded evasive. I wanted to shake him and tell him that anything that upset him was my business— that is what family was for.

"Then, I'm here if you want to talk."

He straightened. "I don't have anything else I need to talk about."

I didn't have to be his brother to know he was lying. "Your security detail hasn't reported any issues to the queen, but your close protection officer, Leo, is certainly holding something back…" I let that hang, but couldn't fail to notice the slight widening of Rune's eyes. Something in that sentence had him wincing, and I wasn't sure if it was mentioning Mother or Leo.

"Why would he; I haven't done anything!?"

"Rune, for God's sake, what did you do? Are you in debt? Is that why the credit card is maxed?" I asked, hoping to get directly to the point. If I asked him outright, he could crumble.

"No." He was still lying.

"Rune…"

"I can handle it," he finally acknowledged.

"That doesn't sound ominous at all."

He shrugged. "At least I didn't run off and get married in Vegas."

I hoped to hell he hadn't done something that was going to cause me the same stress, but I didn't get a chance to question him any further because the door flew open, and a ruffled Harald slipped inside and simply stood there.

"That's my cue to leave," Rune muttered and was out of the room before I could stop him.

"Do you know what is going on with Rune?" I asked Harald. Not only did he stay silent, but he was clearly stressed. "What happened now?"

"It's the archive room, Your Highness. One of the

shelves has given way and the curator has threatened to resign."

Shit, I wished I was buried inside Marquis with nothing else to worry about than getting off. There again, I had to find Marquis at some point and explain to him that his company wasn't the successful bidder, and that might mean no more sex with him ever.

With one curator placated and several boxes of old papers stacked on another shelf, it seemed as if my brain had decided that all I could do was think about Marquis. I found him in the orangery, which had become his favorite place. He was sitting in a wrought iron chair, his face tilted up, eyes closed, a closed book on his chest, *Wuthering Heights*. His thumb was marking a place, but it appeared he was asleep. I sat in a chair next to him, and it hit me that it'd been a long time since I'd just sat in the kind of peace and silence where I had time to think. I rested my hands on the arms of the chair, and Marquis startled me when he took my hand and laced our fingers.

"Penny for your thoughts?" he asked.

"I don't think they're worth that," I said with a smile.

"You looked really deep in thought. Anything you want to talk about?"

If only he knew what was going on in my head. I hardly knew him, but I wanted him all the time. How could a simple hook-up for hot and meaningless sex have become a desire for so much more in this short time? Was it an addiction? Could I be addicted to Marquis and the fact that when I was with him, I didn't have to think about anything but sex? I glanced at him and found him staring at me.

"What?"

"Just looking, Your Highness." He smiled, and all I could think was that I loved the way the smile reached his eyes. He had some kind of power over me I couldn't understand because he was my safe place right now. He never asked me to make decisions or pushed me to make things right. What we had was just us. I was a different person when I was in his arms because he didn't treat me like a prince at all… just a lover. Just a lover?

Prince Antoni—or someone like him—was probably my future, and with my thirtieth birthday looming, it might be closer than I wanted. I had Marquis for as long as he was here, and I was going to make the best of every second of final freedom that I had with him. Only somehow, it wasn't just sex. In fact, we'd enjoyed a lot more of not-having-sex—chatting about our lives, and the weather, and hockey, and snow, and pancakes—and he intrigued me. There was so much more that I wanted with him. I was confused because I wanted to go for walks along the field, show him the best restaurants in the city, and just enjoy his company.

And sex. I wanted more of that. Easy uncomplicated sex.

"Where did you get that scar?" Marquis asked and thumbed the line that marked the back of my right hand.

"I broke a plate when I was seven."

"Oh."

"You sound disappointed."

"I thought perhaps you were in a sword fight over someone's honor." He teased me. "I'm assuming it's part of your princely role to duel."

"Absolutely—I have one booked after lunch."

"I'll hold your coat."

"You'd make a fine second in my totally made-up duel."

We grinned at each other, and I saw the flare of heat in his eyes. It had been a long time since I'd sat and held hands with someone, and I needed a moment when this wasn't about sex or the blazing attraction between us. There would only be a few instances like this when it was just us, clothed, and talking, so I changed the subject immediately.

"Talking of duels, did you know there's an old well in the city, and allegedly, only the royal family knows its location?" I blurted.

He arched a perfect eyebrow, probably wondering why I was changing the subject. "Color me intrigued," he murmured.

"One of my ancestors, Eirik the Second, had this private place outside. of the castle walls where he was having affairs."

"Affairs, plural? I want all the scandalous deets."

I huffed a laugh. "Having affairs outside of marriage is a given in royal life, so it's not as scandalous as you think." His hold on my hand tightened, and he even looked as if he was going to say something, but I forged ahead before we got into a protracted conversation about what my father had done to my mother. "Anyway, the brother of the girl that everyone thought he was seeing challenged him to a duel."

"I'm assuming this was a long, *long* time ago," Marquis said, and there was his perfect smile again.

"1783 to be exact. King Eirik wasn't going to back down, and legend says he fought the brother. They were dueling up and down roads just like in the movies, with lots of heroic leaps and bounds. After disappearing from sight into the residence the king kept for his affairs, they didn't come out for three hours."

"Shit, they killed each other?"

"No. When the bravest soldier in the royal guard decided to investigate what had happened to his king, he found the two men in bed with each other. The legend ends that when the king had to leave to go back to the castle, the young man he'd fought killed himself by jumping into the well on the property."

"What the fuck! I thought this story was going to have a happy ending?"

"Not everything connected to royalty gets a happy ending, you know." I was trying to lighten the intensity in his gaze by joking, but the concept of happy ever after was a long way past a joke. Did I tell him that story to convince him—and myself—that there was nothing more for us than sex?

"Well fuck." Marquis seemed lost for words.

I cleared my throat. "Anyway, the king blocked off the well, then built around it. The knowledge of where it is was passed to me from my mother who'd learned it from her father. It's behind a wall in the museum, and you can only see it if you're standing at the right angle."

"Why is that story not in the history books?"

"You've read our history?"

"Only what's in the library."

"You've been in the library?"

He held up the copy of *Wuthering Heights*. "Harald said it wasn't a first edition, and I could borrow it as long as I didn't take it home with me. He's kind of bossy, but I think he's starting to like me."

"What's not to like? Anyway, I'm done with today." I rolled my neck. "Do you want to go for a walk?"

Marquis leaned in and whispered, "Is that a euphemism for sex?"

I felt lighter for the first time in so many days. "No, it's not a euphemism for sex. It's an actual suggestion for walking around the perimeter of the castle to show you the views."

"You realize it's getting dark, right?" He looked pointedly out at the fjord and the growing gloom of the early evening.

"That's the best time to show you the one place in the city you have to see before you go." He frowned, and I wondered if he felt the same twinge of sadness that I did when I used the word go, so I changed the subject again. "We'll head to the kitchen and see if Magda will let us steal some food."

By the time we headed outside with enough snacks to last us a week, his frown had vanished, and he was back into his typical carefree mode.

We walked away from the castle, reaching the rose garden and the door to the pathway that was private to us on the side of the fjord. The huge oak door with its cast iron hinges had a magical quality to it. Opening it, I gestured him through, making sure I shut it behind us. I wanted to tell him about the fanciful games we played as kids, making up stories about what was behind the door, but that was the kind of thing a man shared with the person they loved—their intended. I couldn't imagine sharing any of this with Prince Antoni, even if I had to marry him one day.

Marquis laced our fingers again, and in companionable silence, we walked for the ten or so minutes it took to get to the lookout. I didn't want to let go of his hand because something so small and insignificant meant safety and security in the gathering darkness, but I told myself it was because I didn't want to let him fall. Liar.

We reached the perfect spot. The breeze off the fjord was chilly. I was glad for the coats we had brought with us. Snuggling together with a blanket over our knees, we munched on pilfered snacks and stared out at the water.

"I can't see much," Marquis admitted.

"Watch this," I said and waved at the fjord.

"Watch what, exactly?"

"You'll see."

Darkness finally met the water, and there was nothing but a million stars above our heads. Then one by one the lights in the castle and the city beyond warmed, and their glow reflected in the water beyond.

"Wow." He gathered me close and placed his arm over my shoulder, and I rested my head on it and inhaled the scent of him. "So beautiful. And so peaceful. I could stay here forever."

"Could you?" A rare hope flared in my chest, and a million scenarios where Marquis was a part of my future sparked to life.

"Sure. I'll definitely come back for visits in the off-season." He pressed a kiss on the top of my head and chuckled. "Anyway, you know I love Magda's cooking."

Disappointment snatched away nebulous hope at his declaration. I don't know what else I could have expected him to say. Perhaps a small part of me that currently felt trapped had thought I had a chance to control my own destiny. Had I been hoping that he'd turn around and vow undying attraction or instant love, promising me to stay forever? Who the hell did I think I was to expect a happy ever after of my own choosing? This was sex and laughter, and quite possibly the start of a friendship, and yes, he could visit and, potentially, we could fuck behind my new husband's back.

After all, it was only what my father did. Maybe *that* was my destiny, despite seeing how it hurt everyone around him. If I said yes to Antoni, was I dooming myself to becoming my father, catting around outside an arranged marriage? Was I even that kind of man? I didn't think so. Was I cursed?

"You're welcome any time."

"Any time?"

"Yeah, but if you don't give me notice, you might have to sleep in the crypt."

ELEVEN

Marquis

A GLORIOUS WEEK LATER, I WAS WAITING FOR AN incoming flight at Norstoe International, wearing a smile that seemed to be plastered to my face of late. It wasn't official that Miller & Miller didn't win the bid, but I had a feeling they had already made their choice. I wanted Kaleb to tell me, not that it mattered, but also, I didn't want him to tell me because then I'd have no reason to stay in Norstoe past the hockey game. And I really wanted to spend my entire summer here.

As another plane landed, this one from London, I passed my wait time by scanning social media and posting a selfie looking all glowy and sated—wearing a slick little beanie with a vest and skinny jeans combo—to pass along to the 1.8 million followers I had on IG.

#norstoesummercharitygame #flightsincoming #hockeyhitsnorstoe #blackandqueer

Several days had passed since the walk around the fjord. Kaleb and I had set the royal sheets ablaze. Every night, he snuck into my room, as it was easier for him to come to me than for me to go to him. Bodyguards tended to get pissy if you tried to sneak into a royal bedchamber with a tube of lube and a dildo. Our nights were spent in bliss, our days neck deep in castle restoration talk.

I pushed aside the worry of being found out and reveled like a starving man who had wandered into a buffet. I'd slept with a few men in my time and more than a few women. Women were just easier to come by in the hockey world. Wheeling puck bunnies started when players were young, trust me. And even though gay rights had come a long way, queer athletes walked a fine line for the most part. Be gay, but not too gay, and all would be well. I tended to balk at that, hence my ever present black and queer hashtag. I wanted that shit in everyone's face when they saw me online. It was who I was. I did not hide things. Well, things other than fucking Prince Kaleb, obviously, but that was for many reasons.

Another flight landing was called. I glanced up, saw that it was from Montréal-Trudeau, and grinned madly. Moral Dunkirk, aka Dunny, had arrived! He was on the first of several incoming flights that I'd signed up to meet. I enjoyed the sight of the big white jet with the red maple leaf rolling into place just a few hundred feet away. I sent a quick text to my father to inform him things were going well and to make sure he had his damn cane, then swallowed down the last of my hot chocolate.

Lifting my backside from the table near a wall of glass in the royal lounge, I stretched to work out the kinks from last night's round of hot and nasty. I'd pulled a few strings —or Kaleb's thick cock—and managed to get all the hockey stars cleared to come through the VIP gate. The same gate that the royal family used when traveling. So, no security checks, quick glances at passports, and limos to whisk us to the castle by the fjord where some of my teammates would be staying. Most of the players were lodging in hotels in the capital city of Husavik, ten minutes from the rink where the game was to be played in three days, but a few of my fellow Rebels had wanted to rough it with the castle dead folks in the motherfucking basement. My teammates were sick.

I gave the woman opening the doors for the incoming flight a wink. She smiled and blushed, then the doorway was filled with a mountain of man, red hair, and flannel.

"M&M!" Dunny bellowed, hefted his carry-on higher on his shoulder, and wrapped me into a bear hug as if he'd not seen me in years. It had been a month since we'd cleaned out our lockers. "You look good." He pounded my back so hard my fillings rattled.

"I always look good," I wheezed and broke free from the ginger giant with the scruffy beard and eternal grin. "You look like you just came down from the mountains. Ever hear of a razor?"

"Bah, who needs razors when you're in the wilds?" He draped an arm around my shoulders and gave the pretty miss at the door a randy wink. She winked back. I had to steer Moral away from the young lady and to our table. He enjoyed the pleasures of both sexes just as I did, only he was more like a bull moose in a rut, where I was a sleek black panther eyeing its sexual quarry. "I just let the playoff beard grow out more. It keeps me warm when I'm out fishing on those chilly Canadian mornings. You said there were lakes to fish here, yes?"

"Yep. Fish to your heart's content." I pushed him into a seat. "Sit, I'll get us something to drink. Another flight from Philly is coming in next hour. Erik Gunnarsson-Lyamin is flying in for the game, then heading home to Sweden to visit with family. His husband is home with the kids nursing that groin pull he suffered in the playoffs, but I snagged a few goalies and a few big names to fill in. It wasn't easy on such short notice, but I think we're going to pull in some nice funds for Kaleb's charity."

"Oh? So, the prince is now Kaleb? I see what you do there." Dunny chuckled and dropped his backside into a chair as someone brought his suitcases to him. Like, right to him, sitting there at the table, as the attendant ran to fetch us more cocoa. With little marshmallows. "Is there something going on with you and the playboy prince?" I arched a brow and tipped the airport worker who had hustled Moral's bags to us. "Ha!" he barked and pointed at me. "You look like you just swallowed a loon turd!"

I shook my head, then chortled. No one could ever stay mad at Dunny for long. He was just too outgoing, too full of life, too adventurous and brimming with good humor to be put out with him. I didn't deny the accusation, I just simply moved the conversation on to other things that I knew Dunny would like to talk about. Like fishing, dogs, hiking, hunting, beer, and hockey. I sat back down to catch up, but kept my lips zipped when it came to me and Kaleb as we waited for another plane with another generous hockey player to touch down in Norstoe. Some things you just couldn't discuss, even if it was with good friends.

It had taken all day and into the night to get all my guests settled into their respective hotels and the castle.

The night of their arrival, we'd spent hours eating, drinking dark lagers, and sitting around the fjord talking hockey until Adler Lockhart had fallen asleep in his chair, tipped to the side, and fell into the fjord. I'd laughed so hard I nearly passed out. Kaleb had checked on us a few times, smiling down at me, his gaze warm and rich as the pastries Magda had fed us at dinner. I found myself looking for the prince now, seeking him out no matter where I was in the rundown heap of rock, and that wasn't at all a good thing. This was a limited engagement run. As soon as the final decision was made, I'd have no reason to linger in Norstoe. I needed to nip the fuzzy feelings now before they could grow from buds of affection into heady blooms of love. Because it sure felt like this thing with Kaleb could career into something deep really quick.

Thankfully, the next day was filled with plumbing talk with Harald and acting as a tour guide of sorts for my friends. I took Dunny to the far end of the fjord so he could fish. Prince Eirik had seen us from the parapets—or wherever future kings spend their days—and had come rushing down, pole in hand, to join Dunny for an hour of wetting his line. The two of them talked like old friends. That was just how Dunny was. He charmed everyone he met. They reeled in a couple of pike, and sent them to Magda to debone and turn into chowder for our evening meal. After doing so, they went their separate ways, His Highness to some important thing or another, and Dunny to check out what the guys were doing in town. I begged off, citing plumbing work, but what I was really hoping to do was sneak off with Kaleb. It had been a whole day since I'd kissed him, and I was jonesing for the man.

I found him in the courtyard with Alexandria, talking in depth and pointing at the kitchen area of the keep. When his gaze met mine, the corners of his mouth twitched, and he excused himself. Alexandria gave me quite the look.

"Is there something that you need?" Kaleb asked, keeping a respectful distance that did nothing to quench the aura of desire swirling around us.

"Yes, you," I replied as a chilly breeze ruffled his thick hair. I longed to get my fingers into the golden mass. "Want to go sightseeing?"

He rolled his lips over his teeth, glanced back at Alexandria, and then gave me an almost imperceptible nod.

"Meet me at the stables."

"Uhm, I don't ride horses. Princes on the other hand…" I leaned in closer to catch the shudder of want coursing over him.

"Give me ten minutes, then go around the back of the castle to the main garage. Pick out a car for us to steal away in. I can give you only an hour, Marquis."

"I'll make do with an hour now." I jogged off to find this garage. Seemed it was hard to miss as it was this massive stone building plunked down on the northern edge of the grounds. Its proximity to the fjord made me wonder if it had been a boathouse at one time. Sliding into the cool interior, I whistled as my sight roamed over luxury cars and SUVs.

I'd just eyeballed a rowdy looking Jeep when Kaleb appeared, looking a bit tense.

"You look like you need a break," I said as I took a step toward him. Then a bodyguard showed up, slinking into the garage like a cat, silent as one too. "Is he coming?" I jerked a thumb at security and Kaleb shrugged. "Well fuck. Can he give us some privacy?"

Kaleb turned to his man. "Lars, can you give us an hour?"

"No, Your Highness, I cannot."

"Sorry." Kaleb sighed. The tension lines around his eyes and mouth were deeper than usual.

"Meh, it's okay. I'm down with someone watching us get jiggy with it."

Lars's eyes flared, but the bastard got into the back of the Jeep anyway.

"Where are we going?" Kaleb asked as he climbed behind the wheel.

"To the mountains. Far away from this castle, hockey players, and the rest of the world," I said, and he was more than happy to make that happen. We roared out of the garage, leaving the keep behind, enjoying the wind swirling around us as we began following the twisting, winding roads that went higher and higher, the crush of city life lessening as small chalets and fields of new grass took the place of blacktop. I queued up one of my playlists, and we ascended into the peaks to Megan Thee Stallion blowing out the open sides of the Jeep. Lars caught my hat when it blew off my head and plunked it back on my skull, keeping his hand on the hat. That made Kaleb laugh aloud.

Up and up we drove, rap and hip-hop vibrating out of the speakers until we crested a rise that leveled off just a bit.

"We have to park here and walk up the rest of the way,"

Kaleb explained. Giving him a nod, I unbuckled and followed him, his hand reaching out to find mine. Lars kept a respectful distance as we made our way up a lush, green knoll thick with wildflowers and grasses that tickled our hips. "My family used to come here quite often when we were children. I suppose it gave Mother and Father a break to simply pack a meal, then turn the four of us wild ones loose."

I smiled at the imagery of Kaleb as a young boy, full of sass and spit, as Dad liked to say. My city shoes weren't made for hiking, but with my prince holding my hand, we managed to crest the hill, a bit winded, and took in the scenery.

My mouth fell open. Majestic snow-capped peaks surrounded us. A small cluster of trees sat off to our left, but otherwise, there was nothing but mountaintops and rich verdant valleys as far as the eye could see.

"I think I finally found a way to silence you," Kaleb joked, his fingers meshed with mine.

"Are there goats around here?" I asked, then gave the meadow a fast look. "I don't trust goats. They have them square devil eyes."

"And nope, that was not a way to silence you. This might work." He stole a fast kiss that set my heart to thumping.

Giddy as a colt, I broke free from his grip, dashing around the meadow, slipping and sliding in my fancy dress shoes, and spinning around in circles as I belted out the opening song from *The Sound of Music* at the top of my lungs. Kaleb laughed and winced at my singing voice—I was no Drake, that was for sure—and then tackled me to the ground, the air leaving me in a rush that he inhaled as his mouth crashed down over mine.

My hat tumbled off my head. His hands began roaming, teasing, loosening the fabric that I'd worked so hard to tuck in, just so, like Tan France taught us. My hips moved under him; the feel of his half hard dick sent sparks to my toes. I ran my tongue over his, delving deeply into his mouth as he pumped against me like a possessed rabbit.

"Fuck me, baby," I beseeched, carding my hands into his hair as I'd wanted to do all day.

"Here on top of the mountain?" he teased, nipping at my lower lip, the sparkle that I loved back in his sky-blue eyes. It had been missing of late. The man carried far too much stress and was still burdened, even with all the sex we'd been having.

"Right here in front of God, the trees, and Lars over there pretending to be interested in them little white flowers." I waved a hand in the direction of the bodyguard, who was bent down inspecting some flora.

"*Edelweiss*," Kaleb murmured before nibbling at the slope of my shoulder. How had he gotten my shirt unbuttoned so fast?

"Oh, you going to start singing songs from that movie as well?" I ground up against him, tugging soundly on his hair to pull his mouth back to mine.

He hummed the lonely goatherd ditty against my lips. I snorted in amusement, then kissed the shit out of him. My hands skimmed down his sides and slipped into his pants to find his cock hard and leaking. His teeth glided over my jaw to my throat. My mouth watered as I worked his cock with slow strokes.

"I wish I had time to take you apart slowly," he growled into my neck, sucking a mark where my shoulder met my throat. The pleasure/pain made my balls contract. "But a fast blowjob will have to do."

He slithered down me like a snake, moving with speed and grace, unzipped my pants and swallowed me down before I could think straight. Lying flat on my back, arms spread, eyes on the bright blue sky, I let Kaleb do to me what he wished. Lars could watch, or Lars could go make a daisy chain. Kaleb fondled my balls, sucking with wild abandon on my cock. Unable to keep my sight on the clouds, I pushed up to my elbows, and there he was, between my legs, my prick stretching his pink lips.

"Oh, holy hell, that's a pretty sight," I gasped, right before he put some pressure on my taint and I blew apart, coating his throat with spunk. He took every bit of it, lapping it up like honey from a comb, cleaning off my flagging cock as I watched through hooded eyes. Then, because he was a princely sort, he tucked me away, zipped my pants, and then shimmied back over me to claim my mouth. My tongue slid around his, and my taste on his tongue was strong and salty. "My turn."

I rolled him to his back, pinned him to the sweet tall grass, and made a buffet out of his body. Every single inch of pale skin I could taste, I tasted. Every bit of tender flesh I could touch, I touched. His cock was thick and heavy when I freed it from his pants. In the same position I was in earlier, he watched me swallow him down, hand wrapped around his root, working him from tip to where his cock sprang from a cloud of yellow curls.

"You're so beautiful," he crooned, his fingers tracing my lips where his cock moved in and out. He began pumping into my throat. Spittle ran down my chin, followed in short order by a rush of cum that I couldn't swallow fast enough. He tasted so good. I sat up, wiped off the corners of my mouth with my hankie and glanced over to see Lars propped up against one of the swaying trees in that copse to our backs. He either didn't see me or pretended not to, but I suspected he was aware of every damn thing that happened to Kaleb on his watch. When my sight returned to my prince, he was smiling up at me in a washed-out goofy way, all the tension gone from his face. I ran my palm over his smooth brow, our gazes locked, my ass resting on my heels. "I'm not sure I can move. Lars may have to carry me to the Jeep."

I spread myself over him, uncaring of where my hat had blown off to. Chest to chest, thigh to thigh, mouth to mouth, I covered him, losing myself in his taste and the feel of all that hard firm muscle under me.

A thousand emotions coursed through me.

Feelings that I had no business feeling, but couldn't seem to keep at bay. This gorgeous man was dangerous. He was working his way into my heart, smile by smile, kindness by kindness. I really needed to step back, slow the roll, and get my head out of my ass. For years, I'd kept my heart safely hidden behind a damn fine Yves St. Laurent vest, but now… shit. Now Kaleb had me bared, my soul exposed, my heart barely hidden inside my ribs.

All he had to do was reach in and pluck it free. And the really scary part was, I'd joyously let him do it.

"I'm late," he said, breaking the moment as if he'd taken a hammer to a vase.

"Sorry, not sorry."

I kissed him with all I had before letting him return to his people and his country. Best to get used to letting him go now, I supposed.

TWELVE

Kaleb

"KALEB, IF I COULD HAVE A PRIVATE MOMENT?"

After dinner, I'd left Marquis with his friends in the orangery. Firstly, because I had work to do, and I couldn't spend time just sitting around chatting about hockey, and secondly, I couldn't bear to see Marquis as anything other than the guy I had sex with. Watching him with his friends, the way they respected him, teased him like brothers, showed me Marquis in another light, and the moment I found myself smiling at one of his friend's jokes, I had to go. I was having too many feelings for him, and it was all wrong.

"Mother." I inclined my head in respect and waited for the latest in what I liked to call mission-Antoni. There is nothing I hadn't heard about him from her. He liked Polo, and his country was just as welcoming to him being gay as mine was for me. And wasn't that lucky?

She hadn't come out and said she needed us to be together, but she was always offering nuggets of information about Antoni, his education, and his family, all of which I knew already. Not only that, but she kept frowning at Marquis, and to be honest, he'd noticed as well. Not that he ever mentioned it, but in her eyes, he was just some guy visiting for work and was another example of me messing with her newest plans to get me and Antoni together. I had to admire her tenacity, though, because she was doing a very good job of painting a future that suited me and my country.

Country being the operative word.

"Antoni's mother and I chatted informally about his visit, and Queen Gosia agrees he should be part of the games, and that it would be good to foster good relations in our somewhat fractious relationship over the southern border. Could you find a space for him?"

I withheld a groan—how could I say no? "Of course," I said after a pause.

"Wonderful. What do you think about putting him in the silver suite for his stay?"

The thing about that particular question was that it wasn't real. I wasn't part of the decision making as to who went where in the palace, that was Harald and his team with input from Mother, so what she was saying was that Antoni *would* be in the silver suite, leaving out the fact that this would result in a very short walk between our rooms. Her matchmaking was right on track with everything I expected.

"Good idea," I lied.

"Harald agrees with me."

"Good." *Well, there you go then.*

"Have you given some thought about what you and Antoni might do when he arrives?"

"You mean apart from saying hello?"

"Kaleb," she warned, and I heard the steely queen tone in her voice, which had replaced the cajoling motherly encouragement.

I winced. "Apologies. But I'll be too busy to do much else other than work on the games, so I don't know what else you're expecting."

"My children are such a worry to me."

"Mother—"

"All I want is for you to be happy. I have no problem with your sister marrying Vincent, after all, he seems to be a good man, although the circumstances of that marriage lacked propriety. Rune is mysterious and off in his own world, and his security detail assures me I have nothing to be concerned about, but I still worry. Then Eirik is balking at attending the next round of border talks. Kaleb, you know it's *his* responsibility to go there and represent our country, but he refuses to do it, and that is worrying me, particularly given your father's history of affairs and errors in diplomatic matters."

This time, I couldn't hold in the wince, and she patted my arm. "I had hoped to rely on all my children to do the right thing."

"This depends on your definition of the 'right thing.'"

"Securing the future of the monarchy. Marrying the right person. Making a family that will actually matter. Eirik is thirty-five and still hasn't settled down. If you could lead by example and achieve one marriage in this family based solidly on duty and responsibility, then maybe Eirik will follow your lead."

Wow. That about summarized every single unspoken

thing that had hovered between me and Mother ever since Father had died in such a media-worthy way. She'd shown pride in me for deciding to take the responsibilities given to me and run with them, but now it appeared that it had culminated into the expectation that I would forge some kind of dynasty with a neighboring country by marrying a readily available gay prince.

I couldn't imagine what Antoni's reaction would be to this and wondered if Queen Gosia would be having the same conversation with him before he arrived in Norstoe.

I wanted to point out that Mother's marriage for duty had made her desperately unhappy. Seeing my father with other women had to be the worst kind of punishment, and an arranged marriage hadn't worked for her, so why would she think it would work for me? And also, why in God's name did she think Eirik would take any notice of what I was doing over political rifts with neighboring countries?

I didn't say any of it, but she was on a roll because she followed up the casual observations with yet another hit.

"You must make the time to treat Antoni as you have done with Mr. Miller. In fact, take him to the fjord after dark to see the city lit up, and to the old town, and have long *chats* in your room."

I caught her steady gaze, and even though she didn't say anything specific about me and Marquis *chatting* in my room—and his room, and anywhere else we could find —the message was clear.

"Have you explained to Ms. Wells that her company's quote has been accepted?"

"Not yet. I will announce that tomorrow first thing."

Because tonight, I had to tell Marquis face-to-face, not in writing, not through his company. I owed him that much, and at least he had his hockey friends to take the sting out of it. The days leading up to this had been slow and long, and filled with careful glances and absolutely no promises for the future. I knew our time was nearly up, and the fact that his company didn't get the quote meant I couldn't entertain the fantasy of him being in the castle with me since it wasn't him that was going to come and fix everything. One fantasy involved me and Marquis—him with a tool belt—but it would have to stay in my head for after he'd left.

"Will that be all?" I asked gently.

She pursed her lips. "Not every arranged marriage has to end up like mine," she murmured, and my chest tightened. "Some marriages born out of need end up in love. Look at your grandparents and all those years they were together, clearly in love." Now my heart hurt—I didn't want my mother to be sad—she deserved love.

"I know."

She opened her arms, and I bent down for her hug, and she kissed my cheek, holding me carefully.

"I'm sorry," she whispered, and before I could ask her for specifics, she'd left, leaving only the fragrance of lavender behind. Was she sorry that she was asking me to escalate a relationship with Antoni? Or was it that she was just as trapped herself? I wish I could hate the message she'd given me, but I'd promised myself that I would be a better prince.

"I'm glad I found you, sir," Harald announced from behind a pillar, scaring the hell out of me.

"What's wrong?" I immediately went to a place where yet another catastrophe had occurred.

"Sir, I regret to inform you that three of the visiting Americans wish to sleep in a rather unusual place tonight." He tilted his chin, but left it there, and I couldn't, for the life of me, think of what he was talking about. "A highly inappropriate place, if you were to ask me."

"What place?"

He closed his eyes briefly and shook his head.

"You won't believe me unless I show you, and you'll have to say no, sir."

"Let me be the judge of that, Harald."

HOCKEY STARS SETTING OUT COTS IN THE CRYPT WASN'T the weirdest thing I'd ever seen, but it was close. I'd joked with Marquis about sleeping in the crypt, but I never imagined anyone would want to do it.

"We have perfectly good bedrooms," I said for what must have been the fifth time, unsure of why exactly these three men felt they needed what they called the full creepy castle experience. I was a little put out, at first, that they'd called my home creepy, but to be fair, parts of the castle *were* beyond eerie. Anyway, now was probably not the time to mention it because the wind was blowing off the fjord and through the crack next to the window, creating this spooky rattling woohooing noise.

I know it did because Marquis had freaked out when he'd heard it two nights ago, and it took me giving him a blowjob to calm him down. Or it was just my excuse because I couldn't get enough of Marquis, and even thinking about him now made me less worried about the amateur ghost hunters I had visiting here. Harald hadn't stayed very long, although he'd made it very clear to our visitors that he'd considered them idiots. I thought they were cool to want to experience something different in life, but I didn't say that in front of him.

"The bedrooms are boring," one of the men said and immediately huffed as if someone had thumped him. "Sorry, Your Highness."

"Not to worry," I replied. "I just hope you will be okay here."

"It's all good," Dunny, the big ginger giant, said, as he plumped up his pillow and lay back on the cot, which I swear whimpered under the weight of him. "I put my phone against the back wall and I'm leaving it recording, just in case."

I don't know what they thought they were going to capture. To my knowledge, we didn't have ghosts in the crypt. I could tell them about the sightings of the gray lady in the attic or mention the icy spots in the great hall, but given Marquis was standing with his hand on the small of my back, and was jumpy, it wasn't fair to explain.

"Why don't you go on ahead," I encouraged him, but he side-eyed me and huffed.

"I'm not leaving you alone with them. Idiots think they're going to see a ghost. I mean, you don't have ghosts, right?" His worried voice caused all three hockey guys to stare at him in disbelief.

"I can feel a ghost in here," Dunny explained and pointed at the roof of the crypt.

"You can?" Marquis's voice had this tremulous quality —for someone who was so levelheaded and confident, he sure had a lot of fears about visitors from the afterlife. It was just another thing about the man that I found charming, and that was dangerous because I'd gone from meaningless sex to finding him endearing for God's sake.

"It's okay, I have ghostbusters on speed dial," Lockhart deadpanned. Moral Dunkirk aka Dunny, Rebels; Adler Lockhart, Railers; and Randy McGinnis, aka Mac, Vancouver, were all idiots. Mac was a goalie and ominously quiet as he stared fixedly at a point on the far wall. Marquis had explained about each person he'd invited, all of whom had said yes. Some were bringing partners or kids, and some were coming on their own. All of them had one thing in common. They were all in some way or another on the queer spectrum. Adler had a partner who worked for the Railers and other teams, Dunny was bi, and Mac was gay. Marquis had told me all of this as we lay in bed over the last few nights. I know he'd been concerned there was a pride theme, but I was out and proud, and my country was inclusive for the most part. Everyone was welcome, particularly Marquis's friends.

I could tell Marquis had a soft spot for Dunny, and that they were close even though they couldn't be further apart in personality. I'd seen enough to know that Dunny was loud and bright and always laughing, taking every challenge thrown at him from catching chips in his mouth to finishing his beer without breathing. He talked about wanting to buy a ticket to go to space or fly like a bird in zero-g. He argued with Marquis that climbing a mountain was fun, and he talked incessantly about his cars. That man loved his cars, and I caught Marquis watching his friend with a soft smile of amusement. For a moment jealousy curled inside me, but Dunny was always looking at other people and never at Marquis, and Marquis was happy just chatting with his friend. There was no sign of attraction or the chance of kissing, so that was okay with me, and thinking that gave me pause for thought. It was possessiveness that gripped me. I had to shove that feeling way down because, soon, Marquis would be gone, and this was just a hookup.

According to Marquis, Lockhart was in a relationship, and Mac was terminally besotted with a friend he wouldn't name—his words not mine. I didn't know about the others that were in the hotel, but I had to stop myself and wonder why I was worried about who Marquis had slept with and who he hadn't.

Just a hookup. Just sex.

Just hot, unimportant, fuck him against the wall, suck him in the bathroom, blow him in the bedroom, sex. Forget the walks on the fjord or the long chats about Norstoe's history or the evenings we sat in silence in the library as we read. None of that meant anything. I had no hold on him, and it was convenient until he went home. That was all it was. So what if last night I felt like some precious thing to him; when he cradled my face and whispered dirty, messy praise, while buried deep inside me.

Was being cherished even a thing when it had been such a short time?

He was just a careful and considerate—hot as fuck—lay. That was all.

"I really don't like this ghost crap," Marquis repeated

softly, and this time he backed away from the crypt door and hovered behind me in the hallway.

"Did you see that?" Adler asked loudly and pointed at the ceiling.

"What?"

"A shadow!" Adler exclaimed.

"Fuck this shit; I'm out of here." Marquis turned and walked so fast that he quickly vanished around the corner to the main corridor.

I pulled the door closed on the crypt and headed in the direction he'd gone, but there was no sign of him. I'd bet a hundred euros that he'd taken a wrong turn and was now lost in the castle. For someone who could collect a no-look pass and score a goal, someone with uncanny control and positional awareness in a hockey game, he had no sense of direction. On instinct, and channeling the panic and fear that had Marquis scurrying away, I headed the opposite direction to the way he should have gone and found him in the library.

"I got lost," he explained unnecessarily. "But I found the library, so it's all good."

He tugged me in for a kiss, and I went willingly, locking my hands behind his head and holding tight. The kiss was everything I wanted, hot and hard enough to turn me on, and gentle enough to make me whimper.

"We have to talk," I said before the kisses turned to more.

"If it's about the ghosts, then I'd rather spend my time kissing—"

"It's not."

"Then what is it about?" He placed his hands on my

hips and snuck in another kiss. I almost gave in and let things go further, but then guilt snuck up on me, and I knew it had to be now or never.

"The decision over the bid…"

He smiled at me, and I was confused. "Ahh, I'm guessing it's not good news for Miller & Miller, which explains that frown you have going on?" He should be at least a little upset, after all, we were sleeping together, right? Didn't he expect to get the deal? Wasn't that the niggling doubt I had in my head as to why he was getting into bed with me?

"Your company's reputation is solid, but at the end of the day it's about money and timely deliverability, and at this time—"

"That's cool," he interrupted. "Can we do some more kissing now?"

He cradled my face and leaned in, but I pushed him back gently. "What? Aren't you angry? Or concerned? Why aren't you trying to get me to change my mind?"

Marquis frowned again, but this time he stepped back until his ass hit a table, he stopped and put on his serious business face. The one where he wasn't readily smiling and joking, but instead, spoke with clarity and experience.

"I assume you did your due diligence, and you decided, based on all the facts you had, that Parson Wells will be the best fit for the multi-million-euro overhaul of your family home, and you didn't choose them, instead of us, solely because we're doing what we're doing?"

Huh? Did he think I'd be biased either way because of the sex? Hell, I thought he'd expect *me* to be biased toward him because of the sex, not to them, and wait, he wasn't upset about losing the bid? Now I was all turned around.

"Of course, I did my due diligence, signed off by two others."

He shrugged and held out a hand that I took before he tugged me closer. "It's all good then."

"But shouldn't you be asking me how you can challenge the decision?"

He shrugged as I took a final step into his arms. "Nope."

"Oh." I crossed my hands behind his back and tilted my head to stare up at him. Business Marquis had gone and in his place was teasing Marquis.

"Want to do some kissing?" he asked with a smirk.

"I have time," I answered with a brief glance at the door where I knew anyone could walk in and demand me to do something for someone. My time wasn't my own, but right now, I was going to make the damn time to kiss Marquis.

So, I did.

But even as we kissed, I couldn't get my mother's words out of my head. This short emotional affair was never meant to last more than the few weeks Marquis was here. It was just sex, and the doubts were there. What did Marquis want from me if he didn't want the contract? Why was he still kissing me? I had responsibilities. I had duties. But most of all, I was running from one fire to the next, dealing with other people's problems, which meant that I never quite took the time to fix things for myself. I eased myself away and went to the sofa, curling up in my favorite spot and gesturing for him to sit in the opposite corner.

"I don't understand," I said after a short pause in which we stared at each other.

"Understand what?"

"Why you're not trying to get me to change my mind over the bid."

He picked at the seam of his pants, brushing it to flatten the crease, and then he nodded and sighed at the same time as if he had the biggest secret and was going to tell me.

"I'm a realist when it comes to business, and we all know that Parson Wells had a better financial package for Norstoe."

"But you're the one out here representing your dad and uncle, won't they be upset?"

"Sure they will." He shrugged as he said that. "I'll get the typical speech about how I messed up and should take things more seriously."

"You took it very seriously," I defended, and he smiled at me.

"Thank you, but I know what they'll say when I get home—how I should begin to accept my career in hockey is nearly over and that I need to look at the next step in my life."

"And I guess the next step is working with your family at Miller & Miller."

"Yeah, it's something I'll probably end up doing at some point. I always knew I'd be the one to take over one day because my cousins aren't capable or remotely interested." His expression was tight as if that admission took something from him. Was it wrong for me to liken what he was facing to being a prince faced with an arranged marriage that would solidify borders between countries? He didn't sound overly enthusiastic about the idea.

"Will you miss hockey when it's all finished?"

"Like a limb. It's been my entire life since I was tiny. I like to think that I make a difference as a queer Black man, out and proud and playing hockey in the public arena. And feeling as if I can make changes, all while I'm doing something I love."

"I guess you can't make as much change in the world fixing pipes." I was trying to lighten the tone, but at first, his serious expression didn't subside, and I thought I'd messed up. Only then he smirked.

"Tell that to me next time you sit on a toilet, and it explodes."

"Fair point," I managed between peals of laughter, which just made him laugh more. We hugged it out as one of us would start to laugh and the other followed. The picture I had in my head of an exploding toilet was enough to shove aside all worries about me and Antoni, or my concerns over Marquis's reaction to not getting the quote. When we finally stopped laughing, and one of us didn't set off again, Marquis kissed me.

"Tell me about you and hockey, stuff that I won't read on all those websites out there."

"You've been looking me up?"

"It's an addiction."

He chuckled softly. "Hockey? That's mostly what is on the Internet. It started off as my hobby, then it was my passion and my purpose. I went from strength to strength as a skater, and through luck, skill, or whatever, I ended up with the Rebels. Jeez, one of the original six teams wanted me, and I was playing hockey for money I didn't need, and that was my forever. I could forget the future, but I knew, one day, it would fall on me to take over from my dad and uncle. After all, they'd scraped and fought their way up for what they had, and no one else in the family was interested or capable. Still, that doesn't mean I want it. I feel guilty most days that I chose hockey, but I can switch between the two worlds, and when I'm in business mode, I'm good at what I do."

"You're being guided by him in a direction you don't really want to go, by forces outside of your control."

"Yeah. But it's first world problems to be so pissed that I have the option of a high paying role at my family's firm," he murmured.

"I know how that feels."

He smiled at me, and I stretched out until my feet were in his lap because he had insanely good hands when it came to massage—in fact, he had insanely good hands while doing a lot of things, which made my cock start to harden. I think I must have returned his smile because I felt lighter.

"I know it sounds dramatic, but for me, it sometimes feels like I'm living in a story that's already been written." Pausing for a bit, I replayed the words in my head. "Yeah, that indeed sounds woefully dramatic... ignore me."

"No, I get it. You feel you have the pressure on you now that you've had the fun side of life. It's time to settle down, take over your role in the family firm, and start the next part of your expected path in life?"

"I'm losing my shit, aren't I? I live in a freaking castle for God's sake. I could have anything I want, go anywhere I want, and here I am sitting in a library full of first editions and the greatest of all books, hosting a pity party for one."

"Nah, I feel you. It seems as if we both have destinies mapped out for us."

"Agreed."

He pressed against my instep, and I nearly purred. Then, he glanced up at me, and I saw something in his eyes that made me so damn sad. "I'm guessing your destiny past this summer doesn't have room for a tall, non-princely Black dude from Detroit?"

"I can't see it," I said with regret, and not a small amount of despair.

He gently moved my foot from his lap and stood up, extending his hand. "Then let's make the most of the nights we have left."

THIRTEEN

Marquis

HOSTING A CHARITY GAME IS A LOT OF WORK.

We'd barely had time to catch our breaths over the following twenty-four hours. It seemed as if there was press everywhere. This was good because the more attention the game got, the more funds raised for charity. But all that press needed faces and famous names. Enter the hockey players. Kaleb appeared once or twice, but he had royal duties to attend to. All I had to do now was hockey. And deal with Antoni. The Prince of Who Cares Just Get the Hell Away From My Man. Which was a whole new set of problems for me to deal with. Jealousy was a new emotion for me. I didn't like it, but I was having trouble containing it, particularly after last night when I came to understand that it was a prince who would stand by Kaleb's side, and not me.

When Prince Antoni—stuck right to Kaleb's side as they entered the rink—came jogging up to me with a wide smile and an outstretched hand, I had a brief period of pure stupid and almost said something. But Dunny elbowed me in the side, and I snapped out of it and shook the man's hand.

"Sorry," I said after removing my glove, then slapping my sweaty palm over his. "I wasn't sure what the proper protocol for offering a skanky hand to a prince was."

Kaleb gave me this sharp, brief look that I ignored. Damn, but Kaleb looked good in his hockey gear. The white jersey with TK on the front and dark blue hockey pants. My team was wearing red sweaters with a blue TM and matching red pants.

His team was Team Kaleb and contained a great deal of European players. Mine was Team Marquis and carried a load of American and Canadian guys. We had lots of goofs and gags planned for the game. Lighthearted nonsense to make the fans laugh. The PR team Kaleb had hired had stressed that we should try to avoid hard hits and aggressive penalties. As we moved through our pre-game media circuits, they kept reminding us it was more for fun and to bring attention to the cause. Sue me if I had to try really hard to act as if I had nothing going on in my head that was any more serious than the charity hockey game.

It's just sex. It was never going to last. I don't have stupid ass feelings for Kaleb.

"Ah, no harm done," Antoni replied graciously and wiped my sweat off on his neatly pressed slacks. Nice slacks too. Sharp creases. Fucker. Be easier to hate the man if he dressed like a pig boy from ye olden days. "I wanted to arrive sooner, but I had something come up in Scotland that needed my attention."

"Golf. It was a golf tournament," Kaleb interjected.

Antoni chuckled softly. "He knows me too well," Antoni said with a warm glance at Kaleb. "I did mention to Kaleb that I'd love to participate if you have room on the roster for another mediocre royal hockey player?"

"You play too?" I asked as other players were hitting the ice for a small warmup with the press corps. Just for pictures and short interviews in the two hours before the game started.

"I do, though not as well as Kaleb here." Kaleb waved off his praise. "I know it's short notice, but I brought my gear. And my donation to the cause is already in the charity's bank account."

Well, fuck me with a cactus. "Of course, we'd love to have you. Dunny, can you take His Majesty to the locker rooms? I'll see if I can get someone to make a sweater with the proper team logo and your name on the back. Which team would you like to join? Mine or Kaleb's?"

Antoni's eyebrow rose slightly. Maybe over the use of Kaleb's given name so intimately by an American commoner? Good. I hope that slid a burdock right into his taint. Come to my game and be all flirty ass prince to my man, then ask me to squeeze you onto my team as if—

"Oh, I'll play with Team Kaleb, of course," Antoni replied, then set off with Dunny to get changed.

Kaleb studied me for the longest time. I could feel his eyes on me as I threw ocular daggers at Antoni's perfectly tailored back. The man knew clothes. Fucker. I wondered who his tailor was, and cursed myself for caring. Antoni was a prince. I wasn't. End of story.

"What?" I asked when I couldn't take the glare any longer.

"Is there some sort of problem with Antoni that we need to address? Again?"

Oh well, wasn't he snippy today? "Nope." I popped the P just to be that way. His sexy jaw clenched momentarily. "I love the guy. Why don't you go take a few laps while I talk with Morgana here?" I spun to face a tiny little reporter with big gray eyes. As Kaleb huffed, then skated off, I spied the words PRINCE—GENTLE CHECKING ONLY written across the back of his jersey. That was too funny. He had nice form too. Stood well on his skates and handled the puck adequately. He lacked real speed, but from what I'd seen during our brief practice last night, he could handle himself on the ice.

Which made me yearn to go knock him into the boards —gently, of course—and kiss him for an hour or two, right in front of Prince Antoni. "What do you think of all this?!" I gushed to the reporter, who was barely staying on her feet. I offered her my arm, smiled charmingly down at her, and then gave her the best and most flirtatious interview I had ever given. My eyes lingered on Kaleb throughout.

ON THE FIRST SHIFT OF THE GAME, ONE OF THE PLAYERS from Team Kaleb hit the ice wearing a Fedora hat and a bright pink suit. A definite jab at me when I'd attended the NHL awards show last year in a vibrant rose-toned suit from Armani with a slick as shit pink hat and cape. I had looked good. Seeing big Rolph Pederson—one of the most feared defensemen in the western conference—skating out to take the faceoff against me in this horrible suit cracked me the hell up. The packed rink hooted in glee.

"Looking good," I snorted as we bent down to fight for the puck.

"I know. I am hot shit," Rolph replied. His hat fell down over his eyes, and I won the faceoff with ease, streaking down the ice to take a prime shot on goal. The goalie snapped it up with ease, then did a funny little dance. Again, the fans went wild. Smiling and shaking my head as I cruised around the back of Team Kaleb's net, I saw Kaleb throwing a long leg over the boards to replace Rolph, who was having major clothing issues. As Rolph went to the locker room to change, I was now facing my lover. He looked so fucking hot in his hockey gear, a thick stubble of gold on his cheeks and jaw, and little sprigs of blond hair sticking out from his helmet. I had to get my hands on him tonight somehow and somewhere, and hope to hell that last night wasn't our final night. I hadn't told my dad that we'd failed on the bid yet, because I knew that as soon as I did, my time here in Norstoe would be over.

Kaleb gave me a quirky little half smile. It was one that always made me weak in the knees, and he knew it because I'd told him.

"Sorry, Your Highness, but hockey usurps cute," I told him, snapping the puck back to Adler Lockhart, who rifled it to one of the forwards from San Diego. I left Kaleb behind in my dust, skating hell bent for leather to be able to pick up a sweet drop pass from Adler and fired it at the net. This time when the Team Kaleb goalie was too busy trying to figure out why Adler was doing a moonwalk toward him, I snuck the puck between his legs. "You need to close that five hole, Piers!" I shouted and got swept into a hug by my teammates.

After the fist bumps along the bench, I took a break, smiling and talking to my teammates, then rinsing the lactic acid from my mouth. That was when Prince Antoni took to the ice. He got some pretty decent applause. His ankles were weak, it seemed, and his stick handling left a bit to be desired. And though this was pure pettiness, his sweater reading PRINCE TWO—SPARE THE FACE lacked any kind of humor. Spare the face. Pfft. His perfect mug could use a scar or two. I had a couple. It gave me character several lovers had said.

"Hey," I hissed about a third of the way through the first of two periods. Dunny looked over at me from above a towel he was using to dry his face. "That Prince Antoni is a bender." That was the hockey term for someone who didn't quite stand in their skates right—their ankles bending left and right.

Dunny drew back as if I'd just called Antoni's mother a dirty word. "M&M," Dunny gasped, lowered his towel, and said it again. "That's a pretty serious accusation."

I waved a hand at the man in question. His ankles *were* bending out. Also, he just sucked at hockey. So, he was a bender. And a duster. Or should be a duster. I seriously did not like the man at all because he could get the man I had to give up on.

"I call them as I see them. If he spent less time making fucking eyes at Kaleb and tied his skates a little tighter, he wouldn't look like such a loser out there." I slapped my helmet onto my head, jumped over the boards with my stick in hand, and made a line change. This was the first time I'd been able to be on the ice with Antoni. He smiled at me all nice and shit. He was playing defense because he obviously lacked the speed and finesse to play center or wing. As a D-man in a charity game, he could barely keep up. Did I mention how much I disliked the dude?

Team Kaleb won the puck, and the pass through the legs to Antoni missed the mark totally. Antoni was too busy making doe eyes at Kaleb probably. When the puck sailed along the dasher, I went after it. And so did Antoni. We met in the corner. Just me, him, and a shoulder check that knocked him off his skates to his highfalutin ass. The check was clean. I grabbed the puck, then passed it to Dunny, who was staring at me as if I'd just body checked a nun. I threw my hands into the air and returned to playing hockey. If Prince Perfect can't take a little check, he should stay off the ice. Out of the corner of my eye, I saw him get up and skate to his bench with a smile that Kaleb did not share. I felt the glower from my prince throughout the rest of the game. A game that we won, causing the opposing team to have to line dance on ice in cowboy hats to "Achy Breaky Heart" as we all sang along.

We raised over one hundred, ninety thousand US dollars for the Norstoe Children's Charity. A good time was had by all.

THAT GOOD TIME HAD BY ALL THOUGHT MIGHT HAVE BEEN premature.

I was sitting alone in the kitchen that evening, eating one of Magda's berry tarts, sipping on some tea, and thumbing through social media, when Kaleb entered the kitchen area. He blew in like a hurricane, his eyes stormy and dark blue.

"We need to talk," he snapped, then folded his arms over his chest and gave me that look. The one that reeked of royal snap-to-it peasant. Which is totally the wrong look and vibe to throw at an American. We tossed tea in Boston harbor and made a certain mad king so mad he spat when he sang. I leaned back in my chair, tossed my phone to the highly buffed table, and cocked one eyebrow.

"You never hear of the word hello?"

"Exactly what the hell is it you want me to do here?"

"I want some peaches." With that, I stood up and walked to the pantry door, slinging it open as if I owned this tumbling heap of rock, and strode into the massive larder after flicking on the lights. "Damn, you people are all about the fruit preserving."

Long thin pantry walls lined with shelves holding jar upon jar upon jar of every kind of conceivable fruit a person would or could ask for.

I looked back over my shoulder when Kaleb entered the pantry and shut the door. He planted his big, strong body in front of the door, crossed his arms, and spread his legs.

"This isn't playtime, Marquis. You could have seriously hurt Antoni with that check. I distinctly recall the rules stating there was to be no checking."

I shrugged and continued my search for peaches. "It's hockey. It was a clean check. He got right up smiling. Why are you humping my leg about this? Where are the peaches? Can't find a damn orange or peach anywhere in this country."

Kaleb pushed around me, grabbed a Mason jar of peaches from the third shelf, then gave me another look that made me want to slap him silly.

"Why did you hit Antoni?"

"Can you just give me my damn peaches?" He shook his head and hid the jar behind his back. I rolled my eyes. "What are we, six years old here?"

"You tell me. I wasn't the one who knocked a man off his skates in a no-contact game just a few hours ago."

"Nowhere in the rules was no-contact mentioned." His face went flat. "It wasn't. It was recommended. And it added some spice and grit to what was becoming a boring game. Can I have the peaches now?"

"No, you cannot have the peaches. We're going to hash this out. Did you check him because you're jealous of him?" I snorted, then held out my hand. Kaleb's sinful mouth tightened. "As I thought. You were jealous."

"Pfft. Right. Like I'm jealous of Prince Perfect. Have you seen me?" I waved my hands at myself. His eyes roamed up and down my body. I was just in jeans and a Henley, but even in such comfortable clothing, I knew I looked good. The flare of his nostrils told me he thought so as well. And yep, right on time, there went my dick, slowly filling up as his eyes roamed over me.

"You dislike him because I spend time with him." I scoffed. He stepped closer, the jar of peaches behind his back, the larder filling with the aroma of his cologne mixed with pheromones. "That's uncalled for. He's a friend. That's all. We understand each other. I have no desire to toss him into the wall and fuck him senseless as I do you every damn time I see you."

Hearing him say all those things made me feel foolish. "Sorry. I just dislike seeing other people coveting what's mine." Ouch, since when did I think Kaleb was mine? How could he be mine, when his family was all over him to marry well?

"Yours?" He placed the peaches on the shelf next to some canned plums. Magda would be mad about that. I was pretty sure she had fruits arranged either by color or alphabetical order.

Okay, now it was time for honesty.

"I wish you were." I slid my fingers around the back of his neck, jerked him to me, chest slamming into chest, lips grinding over lips, and I tongued at his mouth until he opened for me. His fingers bit harshly into my hips. My cock jumped as the taste of him burst to life on my tongue. We pushed and shoved a bit, the kiss randy and wild, but I was able to get him pinned to the larder door, his cheek resting on the hard wood, my teeth on his throat. "I really want to fuck you. Right here in front of the fruit."

"Fuck yes," he huffed, reaching back to grab at my hips, then tugged me into his ass. I growled against his thundering pulse and began fumbling with his pants. "Hurry. Ungh."

I got his pants down and his ass bared to the world. My zipper decided to stick, so I gave it a hard tug which broke several teeth as well as the pull tabby thing.

"Shit." I wiggled the denim down to my knees, stopping only to mouth at Kaleb's bare neck and fondle one tight ass cheek. My cock bounced free so hard it slapped me on the belly. I rutted against him, jamming my cock between his legs. The slick head slid over his hole, which created the most amazing sound deep in his chest. "I'm going to drive all thoughts of Prince Perfect from your mind."

"Prince Perfect," he snorted in amusement. I fumbled in my back pocket, found a condom and a packet of lube, and worked two fingers into his ass. All snorting stopped. He pressed back onto those slick digits. "You need to hurry before someone... ah fuck. Before someone decides to ring down to the... fuck! To the kitchen for a dish of sugared cranberries."

"You just want my cock in you. There ain't no sugared cranberries in this pantry." I eased my fingers out. He kicked free of his trousers and spread himself for me. I nearly blew a nut right then. Prick coated with lube, I eased into him, one hand on his lower back, the other fisted in his golden hair. He moved back to take more and more. Then I bottomed out. His moans were low, guttural, thrumming with want.

"Fuck me. Fuck me. Mark me." I was happy to oblige. I bit down hard on his shoulder where it joined his throat, sucking like a vampire who'd not fed for centuries. My ass began moving, quick hard jerks that pulled me nearly out of that tight, hot channel before I snapped my hips to drive back in. "Oh yes... yes... Marquis."

My name falling from his lips did insane things to me. I drove into him harder, wringing him out with each thrust.

He braced his forearms on the door as I held his head back, baring that luscious throat of his, arched his back, and I fucked him with all I had.

"So close…" he whispered, his voice harsh and thick.

"Fuck, I think I'm falling for you," I muttered against his neck and regretted my honesty instantly. "Let me help you with that, baby." I let go of his hair to grab his cock. I ran the nail of my thumb over the leaking slit. He shuddered and whimpered. With a few quick tugs he was convulsing, hot sticky cum coating my hand. I fucked him with even more vigor now, my orgasm just a few strokes away. He tightened around me, milking my cock, and I drove home. White sparks raced up my spine and my balls emptied into the condom. My lungs were working like bellows as if I'd done ten minutes of straight ice time.

"Oh hell," I gasped, easing out of Kaleb once my legs were sturdy enough to not fold under me. He clung to the door, panting, and then slowly turned to look at me.

"You can't have feelings for me." He looked horrified, which was the last emotion I wanted to see on a lover. "I don't have feelings for you. It's nothing. It's just sex."

"Whatever, Your Highness." I begged to differ because I could see the confusion in his gaze, but yeah, right in this moment it was all about the sex. The man was totally wrecked. Hair standing up, neck red with love marks, eyes sleepy, sticky cock dangling down his thigh. "You look so good like this. All fucked out by me. I'm a possessive prick. I'd apologize, but I can't really do that with sincerity. I am sorry I took it out on Prince Perfect."

"But are you really?" he asked with a certain amount of delight in his hooded gaze. I shrugged and kissed him for another five or so minutes. "You're not sorry at all, are you?"

"A little."

"God you're a terrible liar. What will I do when you're gone?" He smiled and rubbed his thumb along my cheek.

I didn't really want to think about what was coming for us. It hurt too much.

FOURTEEN

Kaleb

HE HAD FEELINGS FOR ME? THAT WAS DANGEROUS. THAT wasn't real and I couldn't let myself have feelings back. When he was gone, he would be *gone* from my thoughts and added to the list of people I'd slept with. I wasn't going to give him another thought.

Why does my heart hurt at the thought of him not being here?

I shouldn't have let him fuck me in the pantry after I'd decided the sex had to end. When I woke up this morning, I'd used the excuse of the hockey event to leave his bed before sunrise, determined to make last night the final time we were together. I hadn't been able to sleep anyway, my thoughts spinning around my future with Antoni and my siblings, but mostly the lust for Marquis that had somehow become more.

But then the games happened, and it was a hugely successful event that the media had lapped up, and we'd raised more money than we'd expected. He'd looked so damn sexy out on the ice, and there was a small part of me that loved the possessive way he'd knocked Antoni to the ground. Still, I didn't go back to his room after the pantry event; instead I took the long winding route back to my study. I passed Eirik's suite of rooms, and then on to the corridors that led to Elsa and Vincent's rooms. Elsa and Vincent were in a tough place, and I didn't have to be her twin to know that things between them were weird. I got the sense that Vincent felt out of place, Elsa was confused, and both were in a bizarre standoff with my mother, the castle staff, the media, hell, even Norstoe itself.

The media hadn't been kind. They'd started off okay, fed the line from us that Elsa and Vincent had fallen in love and that we all knew they wanted a private ceremony because they were so in love. Unfortunately, for all four of the royal children, our lives didn't entirely belong to us, and that was okay. I had a life of privilege, experienced things that some people would never live, and in return, I had a duty to my family and to Norstoe.

Being gay wasn't an issue for the country, that much was true, but should I find my forever man, then there would be a wedding, with media coverage and parades, and all the pomp and circumstance that fueled our tourist industry.

In the past few days, the reaction to Elsa's one true love and her romantic wedding had begun to change, and despite the games, the rumors had refused to go away. The media had photos from a tour of the seedy place where they'd gotten married. It wasn't one of the cutesy Elvis places that had kudos, no it was a back road chapel decorated in a pirate theme complete with an officiant wearing an eyepatch, a fake parrot on his shoulder, and a whole lot of fake flowers. The only claim to fame for the place was that they'd once married the second cousin of a friend of a friend of a Hollywood movie star back in the seventies. Added to that, some of the loudest Norstoe voices in government were questioning the validity of the wedding, and worse, others were demanding a full-on event to mark the marriage as if that was going to somehow prove to everyone that Vincent and Elsa were in love.

I'd thought about a small event here in the castle chapel, possibly a parade, fireworks, a day off to celebrate for the country, but a balls-to-the-wall royal wedding had never been on the cards.

"Your Highness." Vincent stepped out in front of me, and I stopped so suddenly that he had to hold out a hand to support me. Jeez, it wasn't ghosts that frightened me, it was people suddenly appearing from behind stone pillars. He bowed and then straightened. "Can we talk, sir?"

I glanced behind us and, given we were in the middle of the corridor with no one in sight, I nodded, albeit with wariness gripping me. What did he want to say?

"Of course, and please call me Kaleb." I recalled Marquis's question about the bowing and sighed. Bowing in private was kind of ridiculous. "And please, you don't have to bow, when there's no one else to see us, and seriously, maybe never. Okay? You married a princess and in a few weeks you'll be an honest-to-goodness duke, so yeah, hold it back for the big parades, okay?"

He blanched at the word duke, or at least that is what I thought was messing with him, and he worried at his lip in thought. I let him have the few minutes he needed to get his ducks in a row, and after a short while he tugged out his cell, scrolled to something, and passed it to me. The headline was brutal.

"End of the fairy tale?" I read it out loud and sighed. "They went there."

This wasn't a Norstoe media outlet I recognized, but an opinion piece from an overseas news site. Whenever something controversial happened, it was always about the fairy tale, as if being a royal family that was land rich and cash poor was a fairy tale.

I mean, there were no singing candlesticks in this palace that I'd ever seen, and no wild animals turned up at the door and cleaned up for us. The royal family was a business, a solid tourism industry that couldn't afford to lose the fairy tale label. I scanned the article and there was a link to the government website with the clickbait heading "Will Princess Elsa's wedding bankrupt the country?"

"They say what *we* did," Vincent inhaled sharply, "no, what *I* did by letting it happen, will tear apart the royal family and destabilize tourism, and Norstoe will lose everything just because I felt it was okay for me to fall in love with someone I should have never even looked at—"

I placed a hand on his chest to stop him and stared into his wild eyes. I'd seen these headlines before, a lot of them because of my wild and stupid days in Scotland. The British media was brutal, not to mention I'd been a fucking idiot who'd willfully sown so many wild oats I could have harvested acres.

"Are you and Elsa talking about all of this?"

"We try to, but this…" he waved at the phone, "this is all on me. I should have done things properly, not let my heart overrule my head, and now the royal family is in jeopardy, and the country might hate her, and it's all my fault," he murmured and cast a guilty glance at the door to their apartments. "She's… shit… she's…" He slumped against the pillar. "I love her, and I've messed everything up."

I nodded because he *had* messed up everything, but then so had Elsa. And hell, the possibility of a happy future makes the most sensible of people do things they wouldn't normally do. Take the fact that last night I had this irrational rush to kidnap Marquis, find a cabin in the woods, and never come back to the castle. I considered carefully what I needed to say to my poor brother-in-law, and it started with being brutally honest.

"Yes, it's messed up, and yes, you knew what you were doing. Deep down, you both knew that it was the wrong way to do things."

He looked miserable. "I know."

"Her bodyguard, for fuck's sake," I said tiredly. "It's the oldest cliché in the book. It's a movie, and a book, and a goddamn romance novel, but what the two of you have isn't a fairy tale anymore, and it will be years before you can fix that."

"What do we do?"

"Distract. Dissemble. You could give the media and the country what they want, a royal wedding, but it's all wrong and I don't know how to fix it."

The door to their suite opened, and Elsa peered out. She immediately went to Vincent's side, tucking herself under his arm, which he wrapped around her protectively.

"What are you talking about?" she asked, and I saw the

stubborn tilt of her chin and the way she leaned on Vincent for support. "Are you being awful to Vincent?"

"No, we're actually discussing enlarging the chapel ceremony with a more formal celebration, perhaps a blessing," I said, daring him to say otherwise. He caught my gaze, and I blinked at him as if I could telepathically connect to him and tell him not to freak out. I had all these thoughts in my head, about duty, and the country, and how small my sister looked next to Vincent, and how she glanced up at him with so much affection and a smile that spoke volumes. She seemed to love him so much, but I just needed to be sure. "Can I talk to you, Elsa? In private." I had to ask her one question, and the answer might mean everything for the nebulous idea I had in my head.

She opened the door and gestured for me to go in, and when I was inside, just her and me, I leaned against the ancient wood and let all the options that I had settle into a cohesive whole as she waited patiently.

"Tell me how you feel?" I finally asked, and she moved to stand toe to toe with me.

"Now? In hindsight, I feel sorry to have caused all of this and shame at some of what the media is saying. I'm unhappy that, somehow, you're having to deal with the fallout, and—"

"I don't mean all of that. I mean, how do you feel about Vincent?"

She blushed, and her smile was so genuine it lit up her blue eyes with a fire I'd never seen before.

"This is forever for me. I love him. I love the way he makes me feel. It's real."

Tugging her closer, I held her briefly and, then,

released her with a kiss on her head. Elsa was my twin, she was in love, and I could see the truth of the love. I would do anything for her, sacrifice anything for her to be happy, even fall on my sword if needed. I shook Vincent's hand as we let him in and saw the way he couldn't stop staring at Elsa with just as much love as I'd seen in her for him.

I headed straight for Marquis's room instead of my study, and as soon as he saw it was me, he yanked me into a hug.

"I knew you'd come," he muttered against my throat. It would be the last time I held him, the last time we touched, that much was certain. The last thing this family needed was a scandal on top of scandal, and I needed to get my ducks in a row and fix things.

It didn't matter because all Marquis and I had was sex, and it wasn't as if I cared about him in any way.

Liar.

I eased myself away. "We need to talk."

"How about we cuddle instead?" he asked with a smile. "We talked in the pantry."

"No, I can't do that again, this needs to stop now."

"What does?"

"Me fucking you," I said as cruelly as I could manage so that he might hate me and not stare at me with anything like sympathy. God, if he showed me one ounce of pity, I'd crumble like one of the old castle walls. "I've decided about Antoni and my future role in the country—I'm going to talk to Antoni about a mutual arrangement. I'm going to marry him," I announced.

"Okay," he said, all understanding, but his expression was pained. "But can't you—"

"I have a duty to keep things on an even keel."

"But, Kaleb, you don't love him!"

And there it was, the crux of the matter. To show Eirik that an advantageous marriage might work, to take the heat off of Elsa and Vincent. It didn't matter that I didn't love Antoni. It was just how it was. "Love is just a messy by-product of fooling ourselves into thinking we can be happy." Shit. I could hear the words, and I knew I was wrong. I wanted love. I wanted more with Marquis, but I couldn't have it if I chose duty instead.

"That's bullshit, and you know it. I love—"

"I don't love you," I cut him off in case he was about to say something he could never take back. "You and I are just a convenient stop before I settle down and you go home to Detroit. It's nothing but sex. There is no love, and there never can be, Marquis. A knife through the middle of this thing we have is the only way to finish this." His eyes widened, but I had to hurt him just to make him see we were done. We *had* to be done.

This was the only way.

And when I turned and left, he didn't call me back.

FIFTEEN

Marquis

STANDING THERE IN THE DOORWAY OF MY ROOM, MOUTH agape, I stared at Kaleb's back as he stalked off and muttered to himself about something being the way.

I wasn't sure which emotion coursing through me was the strongest: anger or pain. Maybe it was a tie. Whatever. No man dumped all that on me, then walked off as if they'd just put out the motherfucking trash. Fuck that noise. No one chirped me, then skated off. This shitter was at least getting a glove in the face, if not my fist.

I went after him, catching up to him with ease and yanking him around to face me. We stood in front of a massive oil painting of some dour looking medieval woman in a red and blue headdress. She looked the way I felt. Pissed at the world and ready to cut a bitch.

"This is the way? This is the way? What are you, the fucking Mandalorian?" I barked, blocking him off with my body. His jaw firmed.

"Marquis, don't make a scene."

"No!" I snapped and leaned in to get my face real close

to his. Intimidation was my middle name. I was a hockey player after all. "Don't talk in that regal way of yours! I'm not going to stand here and let you look down on me."

"I'm not looking down on you," he argued in a loud whisper, trying, I was sure, not to call attention to our little spat. Fuck. That. I grew up in Detroit. If I had something to say, I said it. And trust me, I had a lot to say. "I'm telling you that what we had was proximity and timing, and I'm asking you to not stir up a commotion over something we knew would end."

Yeah, fine, he had me there. I did know this thing had an expiration date. Like a gallon of milk, but did it have to end so miserably? I mean, truly, is there anything worse than a mouth full of chunky milk after you took a swig from the jug? Not that I did that. Much.

"I'm not making a commotion over the fact that this affair is ending. I've ended lots of relationships. You're not any different than any other summer fling, aside from the fact that you wear a crown."

That made him wince. It also added some starch to his spine. "Well, if I'm not all that special, then this hissy fit that you're having is incredibly ill-advised and frankly beneath you." He was using all the big words, but his expression told me another story.

"Look, fucker, do not talk to me like I'm some hysterical chick trying to cling to her man."

"Sexist much?"

"Fuck you." I so wanted to shove him into the cold stone wall. Or pop him in the nose. Or kiss him one final time. "You don't get to lecture me. And you do not get to end this by dictating where and when and why. If anything, I get to walk off because I'm American and you're not!"

He stared at me in confusion. "What does that even mean?"

"You know what it means." He clearly didn't. Hell, I didn't either, but once a Miller got a good rant going, we were hard-pressed to apply the brakes. "If you need to tell me that this affair has reached its end, fine, do so with some motherfucking class, Your Highness. But do not pass down some royal decree about your duty and your engagement to Prince Perfect and expect me to curtsy like one of your subjects."

"I'm not sure—"

"And one more thing, Your Highness, I'm going home, and I will not be thinking about you or us or that blowjob at the top of the mountain or that time you fucked me in the orangery or when I just boned you in the kitchen pantry. Or the feelings I may or may not have for you."

"Marquis," he whispered. I sucked in a shaky breath and met his gaze. There was so much pain in those Alpine sky eyes that my gut twisted in agony. "It has to be this way. I am sorry. If I wasn't a prince…"

Yeah. Yeah. Duty. Country. Family. I knew all that well. It's what had brought me to Norstoe and into this man's life, arms, and bed. And now it was what would break us apart.

"Can I kiss you one last time?" I asked, reaching out to cup his face. He wanted me to. I could see the yearning in his eyes, but he shook his head. My hand fell to my side.

"That wouldn't be wise, Marquis. If I kissed you, we'd

just end up in bed. It would simply postpone the inevitable. Just let me go with some shred of decency."

Fucker. How dare he be so noble and agonized? "Go then. I need to get out of this country."

He nodded, then stepped around me, his heels clacking on the stone floors, fading away with each step. I did not look back. I kept my eyes pinned on the sour old lady in the beaded headpiece. Only when I could no longer hear his footfalls did I blow out a long, pained breath and head to my room. The others were going back to the States tomorrow. I'd said I was staying for the summer, but that had just exploded in my face.

I had packing to do. And a broken heart to start mending.

I COULD FEEL DUNNY'S GAZE FLICKERING TO ME TIME AND again.

Finally, after a half dozen sideways glances, I forced myself to look up from my phone and caught Dunny studying me with a knitted brow. A jet landed behind him on the tarmac, the sun blinding on the bright metallic plane. The soft soul music piped into the private lounge at the airport, falling on deaf ears. I generally got into good jazz. Jon Batiste, Herbie Hancock, Kamasi Washington, just a few who filled several of my playlists. Today though? Nah. Nothing was cutting through the ache in my chest other than distance.

"You need something?" I enquired, casually thumbing

through Instagram to see what the rich and powerful had been up to overnight.

"Are you okay?" Dunny sat forward, hunching his broad shoulders up to rest his elbows on the knees of his jeans. "You look gutted."

I did? Well, shit. I thought I was handling this breakup well. I looked damn good, having pulled out a rich suit and hat to show a certain someone that I was moving on in my dapper way.

"The plumbing bid went to our competitor," I said, hoping that would be enough to get him from staring at me as if someone had swapped out my head for Pete Davidson's. "I've already gotten pissy-assed texts from my father and uncle about losing such a lucrative bid. I suspect as soon as I walk into the home offices of Miller & Miller, my ass will get royally chewed."

And not the fun royal chewing it had gotten a few nights ago. Fuck. I needed to push all the memories of Kaleb to the back of my mind. What he and I had shared was no more. Sulking over it wouldn't change a thing. He lived in Europe. I lived in America. And he was going to marry Prince Perfect. End of romance. End of story.

"I'm sorry. I thought since you and Kaleb were so tight, he might give the job to you." I gave him a dark look. "What? Don't look at me like that. People give shit to their lovers all the time in the business world."

My mouth fell open for a second. I glanced around, then leaned in closer to Dunny. "Okay, first thing first. You need to keep your voice down." I tossed a quick look at the girl at the counter. She seemed to be engrossed in her work on a desktop and far enough out of range to hear anything. Still…

"Sorry. I forget how loud I am at times." He stroked his beard while giving me a sheepish look.

"How did you know Kaleb and I were hooking up?" I asked softly, angling myself to give the counter girl my back. Another flight landed, a huge blue jet that rolled past us, the sun glinting off the plane and through the wall of glass that separated us from the chaos outside.

"It was obvious. The way you two looked at each other. Like he was prime rib, and you were starving."

"Well, he was prime, no doubt about that." I drew in a long breath, letting it out through pursed lips. "Okay, yeah, we were sleeping together. It was unplanned. Just one of those mad moments where we looked at each other and knew we wanted the other one. It was like… shit, I don't know how to describe it. I'd never felt that kind of pull toward another person before. He was just it, you know?" Dunny nodded and gave me a wan smile. "We hit it right off," I said conspiratorially, my gaze darting to the counter girl and back to my teammate. "It was fucking magical. And hot. Fuck, was it hot."

"That happens. So why did you break up if it was that hot and heavy?"

"He's going to marry Prince Antoni." Saying it out loud didn't make it any better. Not in the least. It tasted rancid.

"Why? That guy was a hoser." Canadian for loser, but it still didn't make me feel any better to hear it. If anything, it made me go into full on defense mode.

"Yeah, he was, but Kaleb isn't looking for a spouse

based on hockey skills. I mean if he was, he would be picking out rings with me." It hit me like a wrecking ball that I'd really like to pick out rings with Kaleb. And buy a place together. Live with the man. Wake up in his arms, fall asleep being the big spoon, and get us a dog. One of the royal ones like the queen owns. We could name the dog Reginald. "I think I might have fallen in love with him," I confessed on a shuddering exhalation.

"Oh shit, Marky, I'm sorry. Did you tell him you loved him? I mean he obviously had feelings for you. Even a big old mountain man Canuck like me could see he was crazy about you."

"Nah, man, I didn't tell him. I didn't even know until right now." I took a second to rest my head in my hands, breath rasping out of me as I battled through that revelation. Dunny rubbed my shoulder. I dropped my hands so that I could give him a wobbly smile of thanks. "Not that it matters anyway. He's in Europe. I'm in the States. And there's the whole engagement to another man thing, which I get." Dunny drew back in surprise. "No, man, I get it. He has a responsibility to his family, his country, and the people that live here. Joining two countries would do wonders for Norstoe. I feel that man. The reason I came over here was to fulfill my responsibility to my family. We went into this thing knowing it was just a fling. And if I was an asshole and let my feelings get involved, then that's on me."

"I don't know, Marky," he mumbled, sitting back and folding his arms over his wide chest. "I mean, I get the whole duty to family and country thing, but what about duty to yourself and your happiness? Though, I've never been in love, mind you, but if I ever do find the right person, I sure as hell am not going to go marry some guy or girl I don't love because of family duty. There has to be a line somewhere, right? I mean… I don't know." He blew out a breath. "Just seems wrong to me to condemn yourself to a life with a person you don't love. How does being miserable make your country better?"

I nodded. What else could I do? Dunny was right. Committing yourself to someone you didn't love was going to be a lifetime of misery for both parties. But Kaleb was a grown man. A prince. And I guess that royal moniker meant that he had to put aside personal desires for the good of the country. Guess we normal people were lucky in that regard. No one gave a shit who we married.

"Well, it's done now, so I wish them all the happiness in the world. Anyway, tell me what you're up to for the rest of the summer." I had to get off this topic before I started sniffling. The pain would subside over time. That was what I'd always told myself when I'd broken things off with other people. They'd get over it. Time heals all wounds. All that placating bullshit. It was all true, but man, when you were suffering through heartbreak, trite words were cold as shit.

Dunny left the deep talk and dove into telling me all about his plans to learn how to fly when he got home to Canada. I nodded along, smiling and making the appropriate sounds when needed, but my mind was a million miles away. I could learn something from having my own heart shattered. The next time I ended a relationship, I could be a little more caring and empathetic. If I came out of this pain with something learned, then the agony would have been worth it. Right?

SIXTEEN

Kaleb

I HAD MISSED MARQUIS EVERY SINGLE SECOND OF EVERY minute since I'd walked away, and worst of all, I still hadn't talked to Antoni after my messed-up decision to sacrifice what I might have had with Marquis for the good of my country.

It'd been a full three days since Marquis left, but I still hadn't the energy or the willpower to do anything about entering a contract with Antoni, who kept trying to talk to me. He was here in the castle because he'd never quite gone home after the hockey event. In fact, he was spending an awful lot of time with Eirik, fishing and chilling in every space I seemed to pass through. I didn't want to talk to him. I didn't want to make any of this real, even if it made complete sense for me to put everything to one side and be the person my country needed me to be, right?

"You've been avoiding me."

Antoni's voice startled me. I'd gone into the library to sit on the sofa because it reminded me of Marquis, and I stupidly couldn't stop thinking about the man. Never did I expect to see Antoni sitting on the edge of the sofa, with an expectant look, as if he'd been waiting for me. I pretended I was coming in for a book and picked the first one I saw on the shelf. *The Complete Works of Shakespeare*.

"I've been trying to talk to you for days," Antoni said.

"I've been kind of busy," I lied.

"My mother has been talking to me about us."

"Oh, yeah, it seems our mothers have been conspiring."

"It turns out mine thinks it would be best for the country if you and I were married. What is your opinion on that?"

"I'm not saying we're heading for a constitutional crisis, but Eirik is doing everything he can to avoid having to talk about taking the throne, the whole Elsa and Vincent wedding in Vegas thing was a shit show, and as for Rune…"

Antoni patted the sofa next to him. "Come and sit down. I think we have things to talk about."

This should have been the time when we decided that, for both countries and both of our families, it was the right thing to do. All I could think about was that I didn't want this at all.

I wanted Marquis. It was as simple as that. And how would that go down? I was here, and he was in the States. I couldn't give up my life for him, and I couldn't expect him to give his life up for me.

"What is it you want to say?" I asked.

"Probably the same thing you want to say to me," Antoni said.

I took a breath. "I think we should get married—"

He huffed, "I think marriage is a bad idea—"

We spoke at the same time, and I blinked at Antoni, not quite sure I'd heard what he said.

"Wait, you don't think it's a good idea?"

Antoni looked down at the floor and, then, back up at me. "You remember that kiss at university? The one in Scotland? The one that tasted of whiskey?"

"I'm not gonna forget that in a hurry," I said without humor. "But it was an okay kiss."

"It wasn't the worst kiss in the world," he said after a pause. "But it was like kissing my brother." He pouted, and when I imagined kissing Eirik or Rune, I joined him in making a small moue of distaste. "There's nothing between us, nothing at all. Apart from friendship based on one shared semester at Uni and one stupid drunk kiss that never felt right. Agreed?"

"Agreed. But if you and I were to get married, it would mean there wouldn't be any more discussions about our southern borders. Not to mention Norstoe needs something positive to latch onto after the Vegas thing, and Eirik is talking about stepping down, abdicating his role for God's sake, and Rune is all over the place."

"Okay, let's look at this rationally. Eirik was born to be the next king. He's only delaying things because he hasn't found the right person to stand next to him. You do know that my cousin Olivia is still in love with him, right?" Antoni enquired.

"She is? It's been a year since they broke up. I thought she hated him after that photo of him and the interior minister went viral."

"Nope, she's stubborn, and he messed up with that photo, but there's some major level pining from Olivia's end. What about Eirik? I mean, he avoids coming to formal events where she might be, and that isn't going to fly when he's king."

I had no idea how Eirik felt about Olivia, or if he regretted their separation because we'd never talked about it. Or rather, I'd never asked him. Hell, we'd all been so caught up with Father dying that things like losing lovers was low on the list. "I know he regrets the photos, but he swears to this day that nothing happened at the springs. I just assumed he was lying, same as Father used to. "But…" I ran out of words, leaving the sentence dangling as I parsed.

"But?"

"I guess if he still loves her and lost her over paparazzi shots taken out of context, then that could explain his constant sour expression and desire to spend his entire life fishing."

Antoni shrugged. "So, between us, we can fix that. Olivia's coming for Elsa's chapel blessing. He can't avoid her all day, and if he does, we'll lock them in a room together." He held out his fist and I bumped it because, if what Antoni said was true, then that was something I could stop worrying about.

"As for Elsa and Vincent, anyone with eyes can see they have a connection that goes beyond the stupidity of getting married without the grand dress and all the pomp and circumstance. You're her twin. She's happy right?"

"Yes, she told me she was," I offered.

"Then why are you trying to fix that?"

"Tourism… the fairy tale…" I was digging for a reason now because when Antoni picked it all apart, it was a small part of a bigger thing. "I don't suppose you have a fix for Rune?"

"I can't help you with Rune, he doesn't really talk to me, apart from asking to borrow money the first day I got here, but let's move on to the important southern borders…"

I glanced up at Antoni as I slipped directly into cautious mode. On the southern borders of Norstoe, the Narender mountain range stood between us and Antoni's country of Leisinden. Norstoe and Leisinden had once been a country united, but an ancient war had put a stop to that. Uniting the countries through us was the best outcome to resolve the ongoing bitterness, and surely not even Antoni could have a solution for that.

"What do you propose?"

He held out his hand. "Make the Narender range neutral territory, co-governed, a nature reserve, independent, whatever, but we fix that between us, me and you, for our generation."

"Our mothers—"

"Would have to learn to live with it. They've already gone nuclear on wanting us married so they could fix the problem of a single mountain range for God's sake. If we can present a different idea, then the pressure is off and we can skip this part of our inherited duty to marry for our countries." He extended his hand again, this time more forcefully, and I finally took it to shake.

"Okay. We can do that."

"But I won't marry you, not that you really want to

marry me. I don't want to marry the first available gay prince and neither do you, right?"

"Agreed."

"And one day, I'm going to marry for love, just like you will. And, if I'm lucky enough to get the man I love to look at me the same way Marquis does you, you bet I'll be getting a ring."

"Sorry?" I blinked at Antoni, not quite making sense of the words. Antoni loved someone. And what was that about the way Marquis looked at me?

"I don't know how you did it, but Marquis was all starry-eyed and loving with you. Surely you can't be that oblivious?"

Turns out I clearly *was* oblivious because I know he said he had feelings for me, and then there was the jealousy thing, but love? He never quite mentioned the L-word, and as soon as he'd started a sentence with "I love," I'd shut him down and never really gave him a chance past telling him I was going to marry Antoni.

Antoni cuffed me around the head and shocked me back to the conversation. "I don't know where you just went, but the look on your face says it all."

"What look? I don't have a look."

"You need to man up and admit that somehow, this summer, you fell for Marquis. You just need to admit it to yourself, decide if you want more, and then go get your man."

We stood, and he bro-hugged me with a casual smile, and when he was just about to leave, it hit me what we'd missed talking about.

"What did you say about Rune?"

"Rune? That he doesn't talk to me much?"

"No, you said he asked to borrow money?"

"Yeah, three days ago, it was a short-term loan. Something about a Porsche?"

"Did you give it to him?"

Antoni shrugged. "I didn't have it to lend and when I told him, he looked utterly destroyed. Must have been one hell of a car."

"And he hasn't asked you for money again?"

Antoni frowned and tilted his head in thought. "You know what? I haven't actually seen him since the hockey game."

I hadn't seen him either, which wasn't strange on the surface, but the last piece of the jigsaw that was my family was eluding me.

"Anyway, back to us being a couple, which we decided was the wrong thing, has a backstory, so I had something to tell you, which might explain things... you know Benny."

"Benny your bodyguard?"

"Well, we're together a lot. I mean a *lot*. I'm not let out of Leisinden without him, okay, so he goes everywhere with me but I kind of had a thing for him and now me and Benny are... y'know..."

"Know what?"

Antoni lowered his voice. "Lovers," he whispered and winked.

Well, that explained the not-marrying-me vibe he had going on.

What is it with people falling for their bodyguards?

SEVENTEEN

Marquis

KNOWING FULL WELL WHAT LAY AHEAD AS SOON AS I stepped into my father's office, I took a day to recuperate at home. Jet lag was a thing. Along with wanting to be well-rested before facing the firing squad. That day helped. Some. It got me some much-needed sleep. My body was pretty good after a down day. My heart? Meh. Still hurting, but it would heal. Eventually. And I'd learned a good lesson about taking the feelings of those left behind after a break-up into consideration. They say we should never stop learning. Well, lesson learned.

When I arrived at the Antietam Office Center around noon, I looked damn good. Professional business attire was the order of the day. From my Fedora to my shiny black shoes, I was working that executive vibe. I snapped a selfie of myself leaning on the hood of my Bugatti and added my standard hashtags.

#feelinggood   #lookinggood   #blackandqueer #detroitproud

Rolling my shoulders to loosen some of the creeping

tension that had settled between my scapulae, I tossed Juan the keys, smiled glibly, and entered the lion's den. On the ride up to face down the Miller brothers, I girded my loins the best I could without donning a cup.

Head high, I passed by Philip at the front desk, pushed on the double doors, and sailed into my father's office as if I owned it. Which I didn't. Yet. I would someday though. My father and uncle were waiting—Dad in his chair behind his desk and Uncle Mike in his wheelchair. Neither man seemed pleased to view me in my glory. Dad's frown was deep. Uncle Mike's face was harder to read, as the stroke that had almost killed him had left the right side of his face slack. Speech was hard for him still, and he had a myriad of other issues as well, but damn the fire in those brown eyes was plain as day.

"Philip, we are not to be disturbed," Dad said into his intercom as the door drifted closed behind me. "Take a seat, Marquis."

I did as told, dropping down into a padded chair facing my father. My uncle's chair rolled over to the desk, then behind it. Ah, right. A concerted front. Excellent. I sighed, crossed one leg over the other, and unbuttoned my olive blazer.

"Can I have a blindfold and a cigarette?" I tossed out. Neither man looked entertained. I sighed. "It was a joke."

"You think this is funny?" Uncle Mike asked, his speech slurred and slow, but perfectly understandable. Both men might be frail now and failing slowly health-wise, but they were sharp as motherfucking rapiers.

"No, sir, I do not," I answered, then folded my hands in my lap.

"Good, because this escapade of yours cost us one of the most lucrative projects to come our way in years," Dad barked. I nodded. Both men in dark suits glowered at me. "What did I tell you before you left?"

"Make sure I have my passport," I quipped. The dark looks grew darker. "Sorry. I'm used to using wisecracks to ease tense situations. You told me to do my research and not flirt with the prince."

"And did you?" Dad asked, his right hand trembling.

Now I could run this one of two ways. I could lie or I could tell the truth. "I did some research and presented Prince Kaleb with a professional and well-thought-out bid. One that you and Uncle Mike approved."

Dad glanced at his brother. Mike grunted. See, I had them there. "Then why did we not get that project? Did you not spend enough time with the prince to win him to our side?"

Oh, Pops, I spent all kinds of time with the prince. He just decided to use another firm *and* get himself another man. Ouch.

A sharp stab of pain sliced between my ribs. "I spent as much time as was feasible with Prince Kaleb. We got on well. He just opted to go with the cheaper bid."

"But Parson Wells Plumbing uses inferior supplies," Uncle Mike grumbled, his thin fingers tapping nervously on the controls for his chair.

"I told Marquis that," Dad replied, then reached up to rub the bridge of his nose. "They're known to do such things."

"Wait. You were telling me the truth?" I sat up, brow knitted.

"Why would I lie?

"I thought you were telling me to exaggerate and be all underhand and shit."

"Miller & Miller does not do that kind of thing, Marquis. What do you take us for?"

"I don't know, maybe because you told me to schmooze the prince?"

"That's business, lying about a competitor is just plain manipulation." The twins exchanged a glance and nodded in pride, but I needed to get them back on track.

"So, for real, Parson Wells Plumbing cuts corners? Uses inferior supplies? Doesn't do the job they're supposed to? Is that what you're saying?"

"Have for years," Mike stated. Dad bobbed his head in agreement.

"Shit." I blew out a long breath, mind racing. I should call Kaleb and let him know about this. But if I did, would it look like sour grapes? "You two have any proof of these allegations?"

Dad and Mike exchanged looks. "Nothing concrete, but we know some sub-contractors that worked for them on various projects. Rumors spread. We could probably track a few of them down if need be. Not sure they'd be willing to sit for a deposition or get involved in anything legal."

"No, no, that's fine. Just reach out. If PWP is involved in underhanded shit, then I'd like to present that to Prince Kaleb. He should be told."

"We'll reach out to the old boys that we know. I'm not sure we'll come up with anything substantial for you to pass along to the prince. Did you and he get close? Would he even listen to you about some wild rumors?" Dad studied me as he spoke.

"We became friendly," I replied and left it at that. That was all anyone needed to know about Kaleb, me, and that wonderful, but far too short, trip to Norstoe.

EIGHTEEN

Kaleb

I STARTED TO TYPE OUT A MESSAGE.

I'm an uncle!

I quickly backspaced. I don't even know why I was sending a text to Marquis, let alone wanting to explain to him how Rune had been in a relationship with Leo, and someone blackmailed them over the existence of Leo's daughter Petra, and exactly how intertwined Rune was with both Leo's and Petra's lives.

Marquis knew about Elsa. He'd understood Eirik's dilemmas, and for some insane reason, it seemed important to me to let him know what was going on with Rune.

I typed some more and read it out loud. "So, it turns out I'm an uncle, well, step-uncle at least. Went hunting Rune down and it turns out Rune is yet another one in love with their bodyguard. Hi name is Leo and he has a kid, and they were being blackmailed, hence all the payouts, and yes, I'm an uncle."

I backspaced again. "You're a fucking idiot," I told my empty room. "He doesn't need to know that."

What I really wanted to send was an apology and an explanation and news about how I'd talked to Antoni. I even started to type it, and then, backspaced the whole lot again.

Marquis was taking too much real estate in my head, and I had to shove him aside and think about the other things I had to focus on. Like controlling the narrative over Rune's new situation, organizing the blessing for Elsa, and making sure that Olivia came for the ceremony, so she and Eirik could reconnect. I almost had too much to think about, but that was okay, because the more I had to focus on, the less chance I got to think about Marquis. I straightened my suit jacket, buttoning the front and smoothing it flat, and stared at myself in the long mirror for several minutes, approving of what I saw as long as I avoided looking at my eyes. They were sad eyes. Stupid ridiculous feelings were filling them and making my head spin, my heart hurt. I pressed a hand to my chest, and finally I met my gaze in the glass.

"I shouldn't have made him leave. I should be my own man. And just because I'm my own man, doesn't mean I'm letting the country down or being irresponsible."

Nodding at my reflection, who didn't seem as convinced as me over what I was saying, I scooped up my phone and pocketed it. It wasn't right to send Marquis messages. I'd made my bed, now I needed to lie in it.

I went to my study via the kitchen for some coffee and muffins since I had skipped breakfast. I wasn't ready to spend a load of time talking about Rune and Leo because seeing the two men together so happy, despite all the troubles to get to this happy ending, was enough to make me want to bash my head against a wall. In frustration, in anger, and with a whole lot of self-pity.

As if he knew the very moment I would end up in the study, Harald was waiting outside. I juggled the coffee and muffin to get out my key, and he followed me into the room.

"Sir, we have to talk."

"What's wrong? If it's anything to do with Rune and Leo, I know things will work their way out. I'm sure of it, the same way as it has for Elsa and Vincent. As long as we can get Olivia to the wedding, I should have Eirik crossed off my list, as well. Then, I'll have nothing left to worry about." I was joking, but Harald's expression didn't change.

"We have an issue," he began carefully. "Parson Wells Plumbing has pierced a pipe in the attic water tank."

I knew that the team from Parson Wells had arrived yesterday, along with the contract manager, Zach, who'd spent an inordinately long time assuring me I'd made the right choice in choosing their company over what he called the "excessively expensive Miller & Miller." I'd had a bad feeling in the pit of my stomach when he said that, as if money was the only thing that was important. This castle was my home. She was beautiful, and I didn't want her hurt, and it wasn't all about the money.

"What did Zach say? He's the contract manager—get him up there."

"I regret to inform you that Mr. Jones did not arrive at the castle this morning. And if I can be brutally honest, only two workmen arrived, and not the promised full crew."

"I'm sorry? They were supposed to start today. Is there an issue? Why isn't the contract manager here? We need to find him."

"If Mr. Jones knows what's good for him, he'll be hiding," Harald muttered. "But, Your Highness, that is the least of our worries. The tapestry room… it's destroyed."

I jogged straight from the study, darting down the corridors and up the one flight of stairs to what we called the tapestry room, which had once been a garderobe. Given Harald's propensity for exaggeration, I didn't expect the chaos facing me when I got there. The room wasn't destroyed, but there was water coming from a hole in the ceiling in the center of the room and falling to the wooden floor, soaking the old rugs. Luckily, it wasn't coming down the walls, so none of the tapestries had gotten wet. And thankfully, the room was mostly bare, in readiness for the work. I noticed Vincent was with a couple of members of the staff, including Magda, and was using his height advantage to reach the top post and bearing the weight of it as they carefully took down the tapestries. It really wasn't a hardship to remove the few remaining pieces, but they were supposed to be taken down by experts, not by people panicking because of a potential flood. A few other staff members were mopping the wooden floor, as I peered up at the ceiling, inspecting the hole.

"Harald? Find Zach—now—the library is directly under here, and we can't let the water seep through the floor." As I moved the bucket that was collecting water to empty it, replacing it with another bucket, the door opened and more staff, armed with blankets and sheets and what looked like old curtains, walked in. After we soaked up all the water, Vincent held the ladder for me as I climbed up to examine the hole. Fortunately, the water had slowed to an ominous repetitive drip. Harald reappeared to assure us that the water hadn't gone into the library, but that didn't comfort me knowing there could be potentially more damage. Marquis had said we should remove the books from the library in precaution, and Zach had dismissed the idea, saying it was unnecessary.

What if all the books were ruined? Why didn't I take Marquis's advice? Too much fucking, not enough thinking, too much sex, too many feelings.

"What did they do in the attic? Who is up there?" I asked Harald, but he didn't have an answer. I headed straight to the attic, with Vincent and Harald hot on my heels, locating the void that was two floors up from the tapestry room. Two men were standing and staring at the pipes that snaked out around the room from a water tank. The space up here was dark and dingy and smelled damp. Parson Wells had confirmed to me that this room was a priority and that many of the problems in the castle were down to slow leaks. I did my research, and it helped that Marquis had said the same thing.

"What happened?" I still wasn't panicking because this was probably a one-off. Accidents happened, but also, where were all the other contractors, and where was Zach? One of the men—as round as he was tall—made his way out from behind the nest of pipes, huffing and puffing.

"It's an old castle. Damn pipes are corroded. You can't expect for there not to be leaks," he snapped at me, defensively. Brandishing a pipe wrench to emphasize each word, he was bright red in the face and clearly pissed off, and it was obvious he had no idea he was speaking to his company's client.

"I respect that it's an old castle," I began carefully. "But any leaks from here make their way down through the tapestry room, which is just above the library. We have books in the library that hold some of the best and worst of our country's history, and I doubt your employer would look kindly on an insurance claim against your work."

The red-faced man took a step closer to me, and in the blink of an eye, Vincent was between us. Red-faced man immediately raised his hands.

"Everything okay, Your Highness?" Vincent asked, and the red-faced man blanched.

"My apologies," he said and sketched a bow. "I'm just as frustrated as you are. I was supposed to have a team of ten at least, and all I have is Jim here, and he's just an apprentice, with more enthusiasm, than common sense."

"I didn't mean to open that pipe," a younger guy said, looking miserable as he tried to bow and curtsy all at the same time. "I didn't expect the water to flood out of the bucket I had under it."

That awful feeling in the pit of my stomach grew worse.

I pinched the bridge of my nose. "I want you to stop… now. Put down your tools and take the rest of the day off, at least until I can talk to your boss."

Jim and the red-faced man eased by us with a cautious

look at Vincent and hurried away, and I turned to face the nest of pipes. The floor was wet, a slick sheet of water that was spreading from under it.

"What can we do?" Vincent asked, then went to a crouch position to examine under the water tank. I joined him by going on my hands and knees and shuffling under so I could lie on my back and try to work out where the leak was coming from. Ignoring the fact I was now soaked to the skin, and goddammit, it stunk of mold under here. I'd been in this same position here recently when I'd shown Marquis around this dark pipe filled space. He commented it was unusual to have so many water pipes in the attic area and proposed that we move all of this to the basement and that initially, it would mean extra money on the quote. I'd balked at that, and he'd offered compromises, but he'd stated, again, that he was standing by his initial assessment. Yet I'd gone with Parson Wells. Fuck.

"I guess it was about money," I said to no one.

"What was? Shit, have you seen this?" I shuffled back even further until only my feet were poking out and stared up at what Vincent had found. Whoever had been under here, and I bet it wasn't the larger red-faced man, but Jim the inexperienced trainee, had taken off the seals and left the pipe open. There was a bucket, but that wasn't going to catch all the water in the tank. Clearly Jim had realized his error, but it had been too late. Hence the flooding. Okay, this had to be an aberration.

Just because this had gone wrong, it didn't mean the whole project was wrong, right?

"Sir?" Harald sounded stressed, and I instinctively

knew that he hadn't found Zach, the one man who was supposed to be here overseeing the allocation of a team of ten, at least, in this one room alone. "Mr. Jones is not in the castle, but—"

"Somebody needs to track down Zach. We need technicians here because if this goes, then the library is in danger. Someone go one floor down. We need something in place if this goes, and we should start emptying the library!"

Water dripped on my face, and I felt around until I found the source, a crack where the pipe threads were compromised. We were not going to get a tight seal from rummaging around under here. There was a commotion beyond the tank, and Vincent scrambled free in full-on bodyguard mode. I wondered if a bodyguard ever stopped being aware of their surroundings.

Vincent wriggled his way back in, and I pressed a hand up against the seal and wondered what the hell to do next.

"Shift over a bit, Your Highness."

My senses went into overload because I recognized the voice and the scent of the man that wouldn't leave my thoughts. A quick glance to the left had me face-to-face with Marquis.

"What are you doing here?" I blinked at him, in shock, the drip on my face getting worse. He didn't answer at first, awkwardly moving onto his side, then he smiled at me.

"Free plumbing, sir."

"You know how to fix this?"

"How else do you think I earned enough money for my hockey habit? I plumbed the hell out of Detroit every vacation before I got the call." He shimmied a little and revealed he had picked up the wrench the red-faced man had brandished. "I have this." He smiled again and leaned into me. Love welled up inside me, so bright and hot that it made my eyes water with emotion. He'd come back, he was saving my castle, and I didn't want him to leave. As he leaned closer, I anticipated the hello kiss, puckering up and ignoring the leak splashing on my nose, but Marquis wasn't going in for a kiss. In fact, he had different ideas. He bent over me and tugged at the giant washer, deftly stopping the leak. "It's not permanent, but it will last until we get a real technician up here. You'll need to talk to Parson Wells about making this a priority when they start."

"It was Parson Wells that caused this, I don't know what they were doing."

He sighed, then laid the wrench on the ground between us. "There is something we need to talk about. It turns out—"

"I love you too," I blurted and grabbed his hand, holding tight before rearing up and smacking my head against the pipe so hard I saw stars. "Fuck," I cursed and closed my eyes.

"Well," Marquis said as he patted my head. "That wasn't exactly what I was going to say."

"Oh, never mind, ignore me, it's been a day and—"

This time he kissed me so hard my toes curled. "But you bet I love you too, Prince Kaleb."

"Oh," I repeated, and this time it was me who started the kiss in the nest of pipes in our attic. Only Harald clearing his throat stopped us, and we scrambled free to find a slickly smiling Zach standing in the doorway. I should have listened to my gut and chosen instinct over cash, and I should have picked Marquis for everything. I stalked over to Zach and pushed a finger in his chest. He tried to move back, but Vincent was a brick wall behind him.

"Your company is fired."

NINETEEN

Marquis

NEVER LET IT BE SAID THAT MEN IN SOGGY SHIRTS covered with plumber's putty don't get any action.

My uncle and father would protest that, and now so would I.

Kaleb and I spent a few hours in that dusty and decidedly haunted attic, fixing the mess that our competitor's ineptitude had caused. Then, he led me to his chambers, locked the door, and proceeded to strip me out of my wet clothes. I returned the favor, kissing every inch of skin that I uncovered all the way down to his navel. It took real control not to suck his balls into my mouth, but I held strong.

When I ran my hands up his back, he twitched. "You've got rough bumps on your hands."

I pulled them back, then held them up. "Damn putty." I sighed. My hard dick nestled nicely into the hollow of his hipbone. "Let me wash this off."

Being the son of a plumber, I should have known a simple soap and water wash wasn't going to remove all of the putty. So, we pulled our pants back on and made the call down to the kitchen in search of mineral spirits. Then, when the can arrived via a confused staff member, we had to scrub the living shit out of our hands to get off the putty. Naked. Seems Kaleb was all about nudity this evening. I could get on board with that thinking.

I wasn't ready to look at my clothes too closely. The Versace shirt I'd worn would be trash. As would the trim fit slacks I'd had on. I'd deal with that loss in the morning.

"I think we should take a shower," Kaleb offered, the smell of mineral spirits thick in his spacious private bath. "Just to make sure that we have all this paint thinner off. I'd not wish for you to kiss me somewhere and taste something unpleasant."

"Baby, there ain't one damn spot on you that tastes bad. Trust me, I know. I've had my tongue all over you." I turned to face him, hands still wet from the sink, and cupped his face. "But I could get into a shower. Long as you fuck me in said shower."

His fingers danced over my hips as his lips twitched. "And here I was going to ask *you* to fuck *me*."

"No law saying we can't do both."

His pupils nearly obliterated his blue eyes. "If there was, I would strike it down."

"Mm, I love it when you talk all regal and shit." I slanted my mouth over his, reveling in the scratch of his beard against my chin. He tasted of hot coffee that Harald had delivered during the repairs and Kaleb. A sweet, manly taste that made my dick throb.

We broke apart long enough to turn on the water in the old bathtub. Claw-footed and quite ornate, but shit, did this place need an update. Fantasies of a massive shower with waterfall heads came to mind as we squeezed into the tub, then pulled the dark blue curtain around us.

"You need to let me redo this bathroom for you," I mumbled as I turned him to face the old faucets while using my leg as a wedge to spread his thighs. "I got ideas."

"As do I, and none of them are about plumbing."

That made me chuckle. Right. Enough thinking about white marble floors, triple water sprays, and pebbles inlaid in the shower walls. It was time to make love to the man I loved. To hell with renovations or how we'd make this long-distance romance work. Right now, we were together. We'd worry over tomorrow later. I turned my full attention to the man sharing the shower with me. Damn shame there weren't any walls to push him up against. There would be when I was done with this damn bathroom. We kissed languidly, enjoying each other at leisure. It had been too long since I'd touched him so intimately.

After a while, he got tired of kissing and wanted more. Easing from my arms, he turned, arched his back like a cat, and offered me his ass. Bent over at the waist, he spread himself open for me. I nearly came right then and there. I had to touch him more.

"You look so good like this," I purred as I rubbed my wet palms up and down his back. Muscles flexed and tightened under my fingertips. "Your body is perfect. Look at you spreading your ass wide for me. You want this?" I poked at his tiny hole with the head of my cock. A low moan floated out of him, filling the steamy area. "You got to say it, Your Highness. Say you want my dick in you."

"Fucking alpha hockey players," he snarled, his head

hanging down, water streaming down his spine and over his shoulders.

"You love it," I countered, reaching down to fumble about on the rack that rested across the back end of the tub. I found shampoo, body wash, and a loofah, then finally the tube of silicone lube that we'd used once before. Back when this was supposedly just about sex. Before I'd fallen madly in love with a prince.

"Yes, I do. I love it," he admitted, moving back to try to get some dick inside him. He was so impatient when it came to my cock in his ass. I fucking loved that about him. "I want your dick in me."

"Shit," I huffed upon realizing I didn't have a condom. "Stay right there. Just like that. Do not move." I patted his ass cheek and jumped out of the shower. I heard him muttering something in his native tongue as I raced into the bedroom, found my slacks, and removed a couple of condoms from my wallet. When I returned, he was still spread open, fingers gripping his ass cheeks, head down, waiting for me. I tossed the extra Trojans to the slim rack holding the bath supplies, gloved up, stepped in, kissed up his spine, and coated my cock with lube. "Now we're ready, baby. Just relax. I know it's big, but you can take it. Easy… oh yeah, that's it." I pressed into him slowly, giving him inch after inch until I was fully seated.

"Fuck. Fuck, oh fuck, that's amazing." Kaleb moaned as he placed his hands on his knees, letting his head drop further forward. Tiny streams of water sluiced down his back, through his hair, and under his ears. I rocked up onto my toes, going as deep as I could get. "More… more of that. Faster and harder."

"Pushy monarchs," I huffed, easing out before slamming back into all that glorious hot tightness. He grunted at the thrust. That lit a fire in me that wasn't going to go out anytime soon. I began pounding him hard, gripping his hips as if holding on for dear life. Balls slapping, we went at it like wild men, primal sounds filling the bathroom along with the harsh slaps of wet skin to wet skin. When I was breathless, I eased out. Kaleb moaned at the loss, whipping his head up to glower at me over his shoulder. A shoulder that carried a nice love bite. "My turn."

I pulled off the condom, chucked it over the oval railing that held the shower curtain, and turned to offer him my ass.

"I want to come buried deep inside you," he said while reaching around me to grab a condom from the bath rack. I nodded, unable to speak, and spread my legs, grasping my ass cheeks just as Kaleb had done earlier. "I'm not going to work you open. Your ass is used to my cock, isn't it, Marquis?"

"Yeah, my ass loves your dick."

He eased in with care. I gasped and groaned, eyes closing, breathing in and out as he stretched me wider and wider, his thick prick gliding home. My knees wanted to buckle, but he held me up, one strong arm around my middle. He bolstered me as he began to move. One long stroke in and out, then another, then another until he was pistoning away like a steam engine. Somewhere along the way, I picked up one leg and rested my foot on the side of the tub, with one hand on the rim of the clawfoot and the other fisting my dick.

"Are you close?" Kaleb asked breathlessly, his cock slamming in and out of me. I made a sound that could have been affirmative. Or it could have been my soul leaving my body. No sooner had he asked, than my balls drew up, and I came with a yelp. Kaleb went deep, then pulled nearly out before giving me that last magnificent thrust that drove him home. Warm cum coated my hand, then washed down the drain as Kaleb pumped his condom full. Soft, sweet words that I didn't understand floated around me, riding the steam, before escaping over our sodden heads. My toes curled around the edge of the tub as I worked my dick. After a bit they relaxed, like the rest of me, as the intensity of my orgasm lessened. A shudder or two rolled out of my center, tingling down to my feet and hands, then he was moving, easing out of me, leaving for just a moment then coming back to me with caresses and kisses. We washed up, taking care of each other as lovers do, lathering each other while sharing sweet tastes and tender touches.

We were still damp when we fell into his massive bed. We lay on our sides, nude, skin speckled with water, the rich smell of his bath wash surrounding us. I stared into lazy sapphire eyes and smiled. He cocked a regal brow as his lips twitched.

"You're pretty amazing," I said, resting my head on one of several pillows, all bearing the royal crest of Norstoe. "I'm so glad I came back. I wanted to tell you about Parson Wells from the get-go, but it would have seemed like sour grapes. As if I were dissing our competitors with rumors while trying to win a bid. Miller

& Miller doesn't do that. We don't have to stoop to ratty ass behavior. Our work speaks for itself."

"I understand and probably would have thought you were making up things to weasel a win for the bid." I nodded, glad he understood even though it didn't make me feel any less guilty about the mess we'd had to fix today. "But enough talk of bidets and pipe fittings. I wish to discuss us, Marquis."

"Okay, I'd like that too."

He studied me closely, his gaze loving and soft. "I love you. I want to be with you always but…" He waved a hand in the air, indicating the room and the castle and probably the country of Norstoe. "For us to be together all the time, one of us will have to move."

"Yeah, that's the issue." I sighed, wiggling my toes under the duvet as a damp wind blew in off the fjord. "I have two years left on my contract with Boston. We're going places. I want to be there for our Cup runs. I love the game."

"I know you do."

"I also love you. And I know you can't just up and leave your country. I don't want you to give up your homelands, your people, your family just for me."

"That's kind. It would be painful, but I would do it." He reached out to run his thumb along my whiskery cheek. God, but his touch made my body come alive.

"I know you would. So, yeah, here we are. We're going to just have to make this long-distance thing work for a couple of years. I can spend summers here. Miller & Miller is looking to branch out into the European market, so there's that aspect of things. When my contract is up, then I'll have another decision to make, but there are options for me."

"Whether to move here or not?" He played with my earlobe as I spoke. I found it really relaxing, as was the warmth of him next to me.

"Yeah. And if I continue playing hockey or take over the reins of the family business; there are leagues here in Europe where I could play if I wanted…"

"Yes, there are. Good ones. And you'd be here in Norstoe."

"And I'd be here in Norstoe. But yeah, that's years away. For now, we have to make the call if we're doing this across the ocean romance thing or not. I'm in. You?"

"I am most certainly in. I'll just take more diplomatic trips to the United States."

"Oh shit, is that what we got going on here? Diplomacy?" I wiggled closer to rub my nose against his. He sniggered and hugged me to him, pressing a few kisses to my closely cropped hair. "I want immunity for when I do stupid shit."

"Officially boyfriends for less than five minutes and he's already asking for favors." He nipped at my shoulder as he slid a leg between mine. We fit together so well. Like puzzle bits. "So, you're asking for leniency from the royal family on a daily basis?"

"Ouch. I don't do stupid shit daily."

"Need I remind you that I've seen you pretending to be Julie Andrews? Also, there was that incident with Farmer Nilsson's milking goats."

"Okay, in my defense, that goat herd was trying to cause me bodily harm. It's not my fault that in my haste to escape, I fell in the stream and lost my hat and shoe." He laughed softly as my head came to rest on his biceps. A yawn broke free, one of those jaw-cracking ones that made your ears pop. Shit, I was exhausted.

"True. Although the goat wearing your hat was humorous, to say the least."

"Sure, laugh. I never found my shoe," I mumbled as he pulled up the goose down covering. It settled on my shoulder and back like a cloud. "That goat herd owes me for one Italian leather loafer. Complete with a penny, which will add a whole cent to the replacement fee."

"I'll be sure to send the good farmer's goats a detailed invoice."

"You do that, Your Highness." I let my eyes drift shut as he drew swirly designs on my scalp. "I love you, Kaleb."

"And I love you. Now rest, my sweet."

I drifted off in his arms. Truly the best place on either side of the Atlantic.

THE OFFICIAL WEDDING WAS PURE POMP.

I freaking loved it. I was styling, profiling, and showing the world that I had me a new boyfriend. I'd really had no intention of stealing the spotlight from the newlyweds—could they be newly wed if they'd already been previously married, I had wondered more than once —but it seemed that one little picture taken by Rune had blown social media wide open. It was a damn fine image. Kaleb and I standing beside the fjord in our wedding finery, holding hands, gazing at each other as if we couldn't get enough of the other. Which was true. We'd been fucking like wild hares ever since we'd reconciled. Maybe it was because we were just that much in love or maybe we were slaking that lust now because in a few weeks I was going to have to head home to start training camp. Whatever the reason we were going at it steadily. So yeah, I had simply posted the image to my IG account with a few lines just for flavor.

I ALWAYS KNEW MY PRINCE WOULD COME, AND HERE HE **is. Love never looked so good on two men as it does on us! @kalebnorstoeson #soinlove #romanceisintheair #blackandqueer #lookinggood**

NOT TEN MINUTES LATER, WE HAD BEEN TRENDING. Looked like love had found every one of the royal children aside from the crown prince. But I had a plan to fix that.

"Are you sure this will work?" Kaleb asked for the tenth time. We lingered outside the small family chapel as a few hundred more images were being snapped of the queen, crown prince, and the new couple.

"Of course it will work." I adjusted my tie and dusted off my lapel.

"But the pantry? I'm not sure that's exactly the sort of quiet place I'd envisioned for them to talk out their issues."

"I seem to recall the pantry being a damn fine romantic place for couples," I whispered just to see him blush. He did. I loved seeing the tips of his ears turn red. "You just get Eirik there and I'll get Lady Olivia. Then cupid will do the rest."

He was about to argue when the wedding photographer scurried out, looking like he'd just run a marathon, and we'd not even gotten to the royal reception yet. He ran past us without even a backward glance.

The queen, Eirik, Vincent, and Elsa emerged. The bride was glowing, the groom smiling, and the queen elegant.

"Eirik, if I could steal you away for just a minute. There's an issue in the kitchen with the winery list," Kaleb tossed out after kissing his sister on the cheek yet again.

"Oh, well, can't Magda—" the heir apparent began.

"This is the billing," Kaleb hurried to say. "It will just be a few minutes. Then, we'll all converge outside for more pictures."

"Ugh, I'm tired of smiling. Can we just get to the food and dancing?" Elsa asked, which got her a chilly look from the queen. "Right. Yes, smile and chin up. Right. Here we go."

Kaleb led Eirik away. The queen gave me a little smile —she was getting used to my face now, since Kaleb had told the family I'd be around a great deal—and left with her personal assistant to freshen up before the next round of picture taking. Elsa and Vincent snuck off as well, which left me to go find Lady Olivia. She was easy to spot once I was outside. A petite blonde woman in a dark blue dress, she was lithe and elegant and currently in discussion with the American envoy to Norstoe, a round turnip sort of man with big ears and far too much nose hair. Why do some men refuse to manscape?

"Lady Olivia, I've been looking all over for you," I said as I closed the distance. Soft music played from a small tent where a DJ was entertaining the elite guests. "Would you mind if I stole her away, Your Ambassadorship?"

He sputtered, but I whisked the beauty away, tucking her tiny hand into the crook of my arm as we entered the orangery.

"Thank you," she whispered as I led her into the castle proper. Large portions were blocked off to the public, and it would be years until the tours could begin again. But Miller & Miller would make sure all the plumbing—from the haunted basement to the parapets—was up to code. And that meant a new bath for Kaleb and me to share. "If I had to hear about his prize-winning eggplants one more time, I might have shoved him into the fjord."

"I'm glad I could save you from grocery chitchat," I replied with a smile. As we walked I made small talk about flowers, birds, horses, dogs, clothes, and Antoni Mackie because everyone should mention Mr. Mackie at least once per day as he is just that fine. We finally arrived in the kitchen, and there stood Kaleb and Eirik. They both looked up from their accounts, Eirik's eyes going wide upon seeing his lady love. "Oh here we go. Hi, guys. Don't mind us. We're going to scour the pantry for jars of spreads and preserves for the honeymoon basket."

Lady Olivia tore her sight from Eirik's to look up at me with confusion. "What is a honeymoon basket?"

"Oh, it's an old American tradition. Started by Betsy

Ross. We pack a basket full of wine and foods so the newlyweds don't starve or become dehydrated while consummating the vows." All three of the others in the kitchen stared at me in disbelief. "It's true. Rumor has it that Martha Washington even started a small basket for the new couple business, but then she had to let it go when George became president and all that."

"Huh," Eirik, Olivia, and Kaleb all said.

"Things were hard for women start-ups back in the day. So yeah, if you all would like to help out, just wander inside there and pick a jar of marmalade for the basket." Eirik and Olivia gave each other wary looks, but slowly stepped into the pantry. Kaleb took a step. I yanked him back, then slammed the door shut.

"Uhm, hello, it's dark in here and something smells rotten. Oh, it's you, Eirik," I heard Olivia say as she tapped on the door.

"Are you sure about this?" Kaleb enquired while we placed our backs to the door. A server rushed in, gave us odd looks, and then grabbed some clean towels and raced back outside. We'd timed it perfectly. All the food was now outside under huge white tents. As was Magda and her castle staff. Probably riding roughshod over the caterers. The head cook had been likened to a gunnery sergeant more than once by Kaleb.

"Yep. Give them some time," I whispered and pulled out my phone to check social media. We could be here for a while.

"Oh, so it's *me* that stinks. Fine. Is that how you wish to be? I was hoping we'd be able to at least be civil," Eirik parried. Olivia fired back. And then the real fireworks began. Kaleb and I winced more than once as the ex-lovers hurled insults back and forth at each other. Things got heated as more personal stuff was revealed. Tears were shed by the sounds. Several times Eirik hammered on the pantry door, demanding to be let out or risk beheading. Kaleb rolled his eyes, and we stayed put for a while longer. Then, amazingly, things grew quiet in the pantry.

"Do you think they've killed each other?" Kaleb asked.

I glanced down at the floor. "There's no puddle of blood seeping out from under the door. Should we peek?"

He nodded, and so we slowly cracked the door and peered around. Eirik had his arms around Olivia, and they were sharing a passionate kiss. I gave Kaleb a wink, eased the door shut, and tiptoed out of the kitchen, with him right behind me.

"Okay, that worked better than I had thought it would," he confessed while we walked through the old castle, hand in hand, smiles wide on our faces. "I hope they're not caught in a compromising position when Magda and the staff return the china and silver settings to the kitchen for cleaning."

"They'll be fine. Today, you are not allowed to worry about anyone else in this castle other than me."

"Why should I worry about you?" He stopped walking and reached for me, tugging me into his arms. "Are you planning on doing something scandalous?"

"Oh yeah, I plan on doing something *extremely* scandalous as soon as we get back to your chambers."

He stole a fast kiss. "We could sneak off now…"

"I like the sound of that."

"Ah here you are. Mother wants you in the orangery

now. Where the hell is Eirik? And why are the bride and groom missing?!" Rune huffed past.

"Check the pantry. I think he was looking for mango preserves for the honeymoon basket," Kaleb replied as we snuggled in the corridor.

"Pantry? What the hell. No, don't tell me. Can someone please locate the bride and groom?!" Rune yelled as he stalked off to find his brother.

"Duty calls." Kaleb sighed. "I'm holding you to that promise of scandalous things after we retire."

"I'll be there. Can you wear your crown again tonight?"

"Only if you wear your jock strap."

"What happens if I don't?"

"Sanctions."

"Like edging?"

"We'll see."

Oh damn. That sounded promising. Who knew international diplomacy could be this damn hot?

Epilogue

Marquis

Two years later

I stood back and surveyed the closet.

Kaleb was beside me, his arms folded over his chest, a look of utter amazement on his handsome, bearded face.

"And you say there is more yet to be unpacked?" His question was the same as it had been a few hours ago when I'd started working on filling up my half of our walk-in closet. Somehow, my half had swallowed up his half and was slowly trying to break free and take over our newly renovated boathouse on the far northern end of Treschow Fjord.

"Yeah." I sighed, pursing my lips as I tried to imagine where we'd put the rest of my clothes. "Plus shoes, hats, and accessories."

"We'll have to have an addition built on next just to

house your clothing," he tossed out, the jibe flavored with good humor. Trust me, the man really wasn't as shocked as he was letting on. He'd helped me move all my shit into the newly minted Lady Josephina House over the past week or two. The man had even commented that someone should phone Brooks Brothers to let them know someone had emptied their inventory. Such a wise ass. I'd not heard him bitch once when we went out, though. He liked me to look my best.

"I thought they would fit. I might have to move your stuff into Prince Igor's room," I teased.

"Funny." He studied the situation intently, stroking his neatly trimmed beard. "We could have adjoining rooms. This way you'd have your own closet."

"I *do* have my own closet," I parried with a wave of the hand at the packed shelves and rods bowing with my suits.

"Hmm." He puzzled for a bit longer. I liked that about him. He was far more pragmatic than I tended to be, which worked well for us. My style was more freewheeling, which led me to leap before looking at times. Not always a bad thing, despite what my father liked to preach. It had gotten me the man of my dreams, as well as a new European team to coach now that my time with the Rebels had come to an end. I was looking forward to being an assistant coach for the Norstoe Moose. "Maybe, I can simply sleep here and dress in another room."

"That sounds like a good idea. Lots of royal folk do that I hear." With that solved, I strolled back into our massive bedroom and sighed at the boxes of shoes and zippered bags yet to be taken care of. "We should hire you a royal dresser. Jesus, where did I get all of this?"

"From every menswear store on every continent." He strolled up to me, took my hand, and led me out onto the patio that overlooked the fjord. Our patio reached out over the water. The supporting structure arched so we could park the paddleboats that Kaleb favored under our centuries-old stone home. "We'll work things out, I'm sure. We could knock out a wall if need be, but I hate to destroy anything if we can avoid it."

The trumpet of a pair of black swans grabbed my attention. I walked to the railing, taking care not to lean on it too heavily. This old place had been close to collapsing when Kaleb had proposed it to me as a place to reside once I'd made the call to move to Norstoe. Between the death of my father and uncle within a year of each other, and blowing out my knee, as well as my ACL, MCL, and PCL, while skiing with Kaleb last year, there seemed to be no reason to stay in the States.

The long-distance romance was brutal, even though we did our best. I bought out my dimwit cousins, sold the American branch of M&M for more money than Norstoe pulls in yearly, and invested in a new plumbing venture here in Europe. S&M Plumbing was named after my father Sly and Uncle Mike, and we hit the ground running. I had to think that Dad would be proud. He'd always wanted me to be part of the business, as well as hungering for that European market. Balancing the plumbing biz with hockey was tricky at times, but I had a great management staff in place, so pretty much now all I did was show up for stockholder meetings and invest the money I was making into various charities and renovating old boathouses.

I'd somehow pulled it off and all it had taken was a blown-out knee and an aching heart. Now that I was here with Kaleb, the pain in my heart had gone away. The knee? Meh. It didn't like the cold Norstoe winters much, but I managed. Kaleb gave *great* knee massages.

"Are you thinking about what to name the cygnets when they hatch?" he asked, sliding up behind me to wrap me in his arms.

"No, not right now. Although Fred, Barney, Wilma, and Betty sound pretty dope to me. Elsa is a name wizard."

He chuckled, his lips resting on the side of my neck. A chilly breeze rustled through the trees surrounding the lake and our little house on the water.

"My sister is far too involved in picking names," he whispered, then kissed my neck right under my ear. "Eirik and Olivia are fully capable of choosing a name for the next prince."

"Well, they better hurry up or that kid will be here, and we'll be calling him Herkimer."

"They have two more months before the baby comes." His lips were soft, his beard scratchy. I drew in a breath of metallic scented air and felt the tension of the move from one country to another leach away. Gazing out at the mountains, the familial castle's parapets could just be seen over the thick pine treetops if one stood on their tiptoes. In the winter, we could view more of the old gal, but now, in early summer, all we could view were a few flapping flags. It was a perfect blend of being close enough to the queen and family, yet far enough away to have privacy. "I'm sure

Mother has a long list of royal names plucked from the annals of our past."

"Eww, dead folk names." I shuddered and he snuggled up closer.

"When do you want to start on our family?" he asked, his voice a warm, sweet puff of air dancing over my ear. "Olivia is expecting, Elsa is expecting, Rune already has a child. It's our turn to add a prince or princess to the lineage papers."

"We'd have to get married first, and since we've not done that…" I let it dangle. This was a common talk over the past year. Marriage had been an impossible dream when he'd been in Norstoe, and I was in Boston or Detroit.

"Well, we're both here now. You'll soon be a new citizen of Norstoe."

"Dual citizenship," I reminded him.

"Of course, half and half." I nodded smugly. "Be that as it may, you will be a citizen of this country, which Mother was adamant about. Once that is official, we should get married and have a child."

"I'm down with all that, but someone has to ask someone else to marry them first. And given that no one has asked anyone…"

"Forgive me. I was too busy moving the man that I love beyond reason and his ten thousand hats into our new, but historically older than shit, home." I snorted, then allowed him to spin me to face him. His eyes glowed with humor and love. "Will you marry me and have my babies?"

"You best sit down with the queen and have that birds and the bees talk, Your Highness." I wrapped my arms around his middle, pulling him flush to me, enjoying the heat that poured off him. The man was like a walking furnace, which was a blessing, living here when the snow flies.

"I'll do that tomorrow." He cupped my face in his hands. His palms were toasty. From around the sharp bend in the fjord one swan called to the other, the loud honks of the cob—the male—to his mate—the pen—sitting on a nest nearby rang out. "Will you marry me? I'm quite the catch. And I come with my own rickety boathouse, two swans that would rather bite than talk, and a family that spends far too much time trying to stick their noses where they don't belong. Overall, now that I think of it, I might not be that much of a catch after all."

"You're one hell of a catch. Minus the nasty swans and dead people in the basement. That's just weird as shit."

He dropped a kiss on my nose. "So, was that a yes?"

"It's a yes. Now, go have that talk with your mother."

"Tomorrow. Tonight, I plan on making love to my fiancé."

His mouth slanted over mine. I held him close and kissed him back with all the love I had for him flowing freely. Guess fairy tales really do come true.

And I don't even own glass slippers.

THE END

What's next for the Rebels?

Blade (Boston Rebels 5)

Love doesn't have a formula. It's messy, unpredictable, and impossible to control for the shy billionaire inventor and the hockey player who believes he's lost everything.

Moral "Dunny" Dunkirk has a passion for life. A robust outdoorsman, lover of life, and one of the Boston Rebels fan favorites, Dunny has always embraced excitement and the drive to try new things. During his inaugural flight behind the controls of a small plane, the fates decide to test his mettle in a way that he had never envisioned. When everything crashes down around him, he's lost in depression and alone in his cabin, facing an existence that is nothing like the one he previously led. Desperate to find some hope, Dunny reaches out to The Harvey Foundation who might be able to help, and he soon finds himself being lifted out of the pit of darkness he'd fallen into one shy, quirky, uplifting smile at a time.

Accidental billionaire and eccentric inventor Cooper Harvey is only happy in the seclusion of his lab, creating new and wonderful things he is sure will make the world a better place. Other than being blackmailed into spending every fourth Sunday at his PA's house for dinner, he avoids the chaos of the world, and if that means no social life, then he's okay with that. In the most splendid isolation money can buy, he escapes the complicated and difficult emotions surrounding attraction, and his single-minded focus means that sex and love are way down his list. When his latest invention reaches the testing stage, he would normally hand it over to his development team, but a chance meeting with the test subject makes him rethink. Something about the hockey player who'd lost it all makes him think life isn't all about measured chemical reactions, and sometimes it's just about the craziness of love.

Free Reads

Please note - in all of these free stories, there will be some spoilers for the main series books.

Railers Short Stories

Volume 1 | Volume 2

LA Storm

Sparkle

The Colts - AHL Short Stories

Pucks & Percentages

Breakaway

Making the Save

Standalone

Waiting for Christmas

When hockey wunderkind Tennant Rowe meets his new coach, he knows he's in trouble. Jared Madsen is nine years older than Tennant, impossibly attractive, and — worst of all — his brother's off-limits best friend. Is their chemistry worth the risk?

Changing Lines (Railers 1)

Can Tennant show Jared that age is just a number, and that love is all that matters?

The Rowe Brothers are famous hockey hotshots, but as the youngest of the trio, Tennant has always had to play against his brothers' reputations. To get out of their shadows, and against their advice, he accepts a trade to the Harrisburg Railers, where he runs into Jared Madsen. Mads is an old family friend and his brother's one-time teammate. Mads is Tennant's new coach. And Mads is the sexiest thing he's ever laid eyes on.

Jared Madsen's hockey career was cut short by a fault in his heart, but coaching keeps him close to the game. When Ten is traded to the team, his carefully organized world is thrown into chaos. Nine years his junior and his best friend's brother, he knows Ten is strictly off-limits, but as soon as he sees Ten's moves, on and off the ice, he knows that his heart could get him into trouble again.

Changing Lines

Harrisburg Railers (Hockey Romance)

1. Changing Lines
2. First Season
3. Deep Edge
4. Poke Check
5. Last Defense
6. Goal Line
7. Neutral Zone
8. Hat Trick
9. Save The Date
10. Baby Makes Three
11. Rivals
12. Perfect Gifts
13. Family First

Meet the men of Owatonna University's hockey team

Ryker (Owatonna U, 1)

Ryker

Ryker is hockey royalty, Jacob is a poor country boy. Can two vastly different people find common ground and become the men they want to be?

Ryker comes from a long line of championship-winning hockey players. Playing college hockey to develop his game is his only focus, and nothing will stand in the way of him working to become the best player. He has no room for relationships, people who point out his flaws, or anyone who calls him on his dreams. He certainly has no place for love, and meeting Jacob is nothing but a useful distraction on the side. After all trying to get his Owatonna Eagles teammate into bed is less work and more play. When tragedy rocks his family, his charmed life crumbles, and the only person he can turn to is the same one who claims to hate him.

Jacob Benson has only known hard work and stifling conservative values his whole life. Born and raised in the small rural community of Eden Crossing, Minnesota, he's the only son of a hard-working but struggling dairy farming family. Jacob is using his skills in hockey to finance his way to an agricultural science degree. These four years at Owatonna U. will probably be the only time he has to enjoy life, gain acceptance about his sexuality, and live openly before his inevitable return to the farm. Running into a pretty rich boy like Ryker Madsen is putting a damper on his enjoyment of life away from home. Ryker's flip, conceited, carefree attitude grates on Jacob's every nerve. So why, if Ryker is everything he dislikes, does he want nothing more than to explore the sinful dreams that his annoying teammate stars in every night?

Ryker

Owatonna U Hockey (Hockey Romance)

1. Ryker
2. Scott
3. Benoit

Coast to Coast (Arizona Raptors 1)

Coast To Coast

When opposites attract, this bottom-of-the-league team will never be the same again.

A stipulation in his father's will forces Mark back into the arms of a family that disowned him and leaves him one-third owner of a hockey team facing financial ruin. He doesn't even watch hockey, let alone like it, and wants nothing more than to head back to New York. Then there's the new coach, a stubborn, opinionated, irritating man with superiority issues and questionable music taste. Butting heads with Rowen becomes the new normal, but it comes with passionate debate and an all-consuming lust.

Challenged to rebuild one of the worst teams in the league into a future cup contender, Rowen can't pass up the opportunity. Never in his twenty years of hockey has he ever seen a team managed so badly or coached players overflowing with resentment and bigotry. Yet there's something about this team and this city that compels him to roll up his sleeves and start dismantling. If only Mark, one of three siblings who now own the Raptors, wasn't so damned rock-headed yet so damned appealing his job might be easier. It doesn't look like either is willing to give in, but one night in a dark, desert hotel changes everything.

Coast To Coast

Arizona Raptors (Hockey Romance)

1. Coast To Coast
2. Across the Pond
3. Shadow and Light
4. Sugar and Ice
5. School and Rock

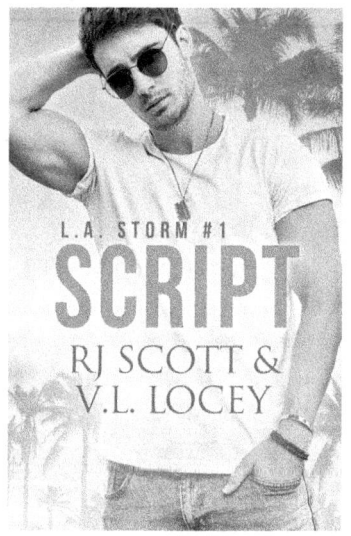

Script (LA Storm, 1)

Script

Hollywood A-lister Finn might be Canadian, but he needs Cameron to show him how to hockey.

Actor Finn Kerrigan is at a crossroads. After growing up a soap star, then starring in a hugely successful trilogy of action movies, he's finally given the chance to read a heartfelt and passionate script that could change his life forever. The role would be enough for people to see him as a serious actor, and maybe even win him an award or two (and no, a golden raspberry award for his action movies doesn't count). Once established as a serious actor he's sure he can come out of the closet and finally live his truth. When he lies to get the part of a hockey player on a struggling team, he suddenly has nowhere to hide. He might be Canadian, but the last time he skated he was ten, and no, he doesn't have hockey in his blood. With only a month until filming starts, he about to be exposed, but partnered with a player who's supposed to be giving him tips, he doesn't realize how many of his secrets will come to light. Falling in lust, one heated kiss at a time, is inevitable, but giving Cameron up at the end of the shoot could break his heart.

Cameron Chavkin is the face of the LA Storm. And the body, and the hair, and the smile. He's at the prime of his career, men and women want to be with him, and he's skating better than he ever has before. His house sits next to a famous rock star's mansion, his garage is filled with expensive cars, and he's even been asked to mentor a once-famous actor in a new hockey movie. Life is pretty sweet. Until the bad boy of hockey meets Finn, a man on the edge with more secrets than Cameron has endorsements. Knowing better than to get involved, Cameron is swept up despite himself, and when it's time to say goodbye to the Storm's most eligible bachelor is finding it hard to follow the script.

Script

LA Storm

1. Script
2. Second
3. Shield
4. Spiral

Chesterford Coyotes, Young Adult
Romance

Off The Ice (Chesterford Coyotes, 1)

Off The Ice

**A coming-of-age love story with high school, hockey rivalry,
friendship, family, and coming out.**

Soren's life changes in an instant when he and his younger
brother are adopted by hockey royalty. Making sense of his new
life is hard enough, but when he's enrolled in a private school it
means facing a whole new set of problems. Navigating
friendship, family, and hockey is one thing, but being attracted to
the boy who vexes him is a whole new thing.

Felix has a reputation to protect. He's the kid who seems to have everything but looks can be deceiving. Spinning lies about his perfect life, he's created a fantasy world that even he has started to believe. Only, it's not long before everything crumbles, all of his pretty lies are revealed, and only his closest rival sees through his pain and stands by him.

Fighting is easy, friendship is hard, but love is everything.

Off The Ice

Chesterford Coyotes

1. Off The Ice
2. On Thin Ice
3. *Dance on Ice*

Also By RJ Scott

For a full list of ebooks and links please scan the code above or visit rjscott.co.uk/rjbooks

Meet RJ Scott

RJ discovered romance in books at a very young age and realized that if there wasn't romance on the page, she could create it in her head. With over one hundred and fifty books published, she is a full time author of gay romance.

She lives and works out of her home in the beautiful English countryside, spends her spare time reading, watching films, and enjoying time with her family.

The last time she had a week's break from writing she didn't like it one little bit and has yet to meet a box of chocolates she couldn't defeat.

www.rjscott.co.uk | rj@rjscott.co.uk

NEWSLETTER - rjscott.co.uk/rjnews

facebook.com/author.rjscott

x.com/Rjscott_author

instagram.com/rjscott_author

amazon.com/author/rj-scott

bookbub.com/authors/rj-scott

goodreads.com/rjscott

pinterest.com/rjscottauthor

Also By VL Locey

For a full list of ebooks and links please scan the code above or
visit vlloccy.com/stories-from-vl-locey

Meet V.L. Locey

V.L. Locey loves worn jeans, yoga, belly laughs, walking, reading and writing lusty tales, Greek mythology, the New York Rangers, comic books, and coffee.

(Not necessarily in that order.)

She shares her life with her husband, her daughter, one dog, two cats, a flock of assorted domestic fowl, and two Jersey steers.

When not writing spicy romances, she enjoys spending her day with her menagerie in the rolling hills of Pennsylvania with a cup of fresh java in hand.

vllocey.com
vicki@vllocey.com

Newsletter - vllocey.com/newsletter

facebook.com/V.L.Locey
x.com/vllocey
instagram.com/vl_locey
bookbub.com/authors/v-l-locey
goodreads.com/vllocey
pinterest.com/vllocey